REDEMPTION

THE PRIEST and PROSTITUTE

Jacob Knorpp

Redemption is dedicated to my lovely wife, Renee. She was my encouragement as I wrote these pages. Thank you, sweetheart!

REDEMPTION

By Jacob Knorpp

PART 1

Chapter One

———

Sheila was drenched in sweat, partly from the humid night air and partly from her profession that had enslaved her. The job now finished, she shoved his five-foot eight-inch, two-hundred fifty pound frame from her body and picked up her fee from the coffee table. She quickly put her work clothes back on and reached for the door.

"You leaving so soon?" her recent business deal asked.

"Haven't you ever heard 'time is money'?" Sheila retorted over her shoulder as she walked out to drum up another customer. "Make sure you're out in ten minutes, and straighten up that bed."

The hot night air hit her like a furnace blast. *My God, it feels like I've skipped the formality of dying and just went straight to hell,* Sheila thought as she wiped at more sweat, this time from her face. As she walked along to her customary spot, she found herself lost in her thoughts in an increasingly familiar territory. Her son, now seven years old, had been to every specialist that she could afford, but no one seemed to give her any hope that the cancer could be reversed. A rare brain cancer, they said. She had quit her "real" job to take care of him, and there had never been any insurance in the picture. Public assistance wouldn't pay for the kind of experimental treatments he now needed. What little money she'd saved was long used up. The good-for-nothing 'father' of the boy had left after he realized that she was pregnant. With no other family she could turn to, Sheila had taken matters into her own hands.

Her new "profession" paid very well. She laughed under her breath as she compared her current job to an advertisement that she had read on the wall while standing in line at her old hometown welfare office. It had said, "Be your own boss: work as hard as you want; make as much as you want." There was an exotic vacation to be won if you produced enough business. That was a much more innocent time. *Well, I wonder if I've produced enough business yet*, she thought wryly. She'd definitely done enough "deals." She had twenty-five thousand dollars more to go for a new, experimental treatment for Chance at the Miami Children's Hospital. The success rate was just forty percent, but it was the last avenue for Sheila. Her son had been given just a few more months to live and nothing was going to stand in her way to give Chance every opportunity for life. He was the only thing that mattered to her. If she needed to use her body to try to save his, then *by God, let's get the cash register ringing.*

"Desperate times call for desperate measures," her mother had always told her. Her mother was killed in an auto accident when Sheila was ten. Her father was an alcoholic who drank himself to death shortly thereafter. She was raised by her aunt and set out on her own after finishing high school. Sheila had never found her footing. Working as a waitress, she had made ends meet. That had all changed the day of Chance's diagnosis. Her world had revolved around her son. He had been all that she'd had - a sense of normalcy that she'd desperately needed. Now, her world was a lonely dark night with vultures encircling.

The only glimmer of light in her life had come recently when a most unusual meeting had occurred at her usual advertising area. A priest by the name of Tom had come by and the two had visited briefly. Ready for some lecture on morality, Sheila was left speechless by the encounter. She could only remember three things from their conversation. He had insisted that she call him "Tom," he had kind ocean blue eyes, and he had given her five hundred dollars, with the additional promise that she could room at the church if she needed. "Probably just hoping for a little extra bonus from me," Sheila had reasoned the kindness away. *"Since the pedophiles can't get the altar boys anymore, I guess now they're coming after us."* She made a mental note to tell Tom this if he ever had the nerve to come to her part of town again.

Chapter Two

"Unscrew that shut-off valve or this sucker's gonna blow!" yelled Harvey. Harvey was going on his seventh year as a platform supervisor at Goldman Oil. His six-four frame was chiseled by his ten years of hard work at the company. At twenty-eight years old, he was already the best supervisor the company had. "Why can't they ever send me someone with any common sense?" Harvey was bellowing. "Do you know how close you came to destroying this whole rig? Damn close! Now get off my platform and go work on your tan." The newbie had put the whole crew's life in danger just because of his daydreaming. Harvey commanded a tight ship and just one wrong move in a profession like this would land everyone a mile from the rig in Never-Never Land. It was getting harder to find good help these days, and it seemed like more and more mommas' boys were coming his way looking for work. With most of them, their mommas would've done a much better job. This current freshman had been with his crew only two weeks, but Harvey had known it was only a matter of time until he was going back home. He only wished it was two weeks ago. Harvey had a flawless safety record since his promotion to supervisor seven years ago and he wasn't going to let this rookie get another chance at ruining it. The previous supervisor, in Harvey's first few years with the company, had started drinking on the job and had overseen several accidents. In one mishap, a veteran with Goldman had lost his life. That was when Harvey, with only three years of experience, was chosen to be the new crew boss. Words like "responsible," and "dedicated," labeled him when he was promoted. Harvey had committed himself one hundred per-cent to being successful with the confidence the company had invested in him. He worked sixty to seventy hours a week and had not taken a vaca-tion to date. The lack of a female relationship in his life was definitely not due to any lack of female interest. When Harvey was doing personal busi-ness in town, he always caught the ladies' atten-tion. His void of female companionship also had nothing to do with a taste for the same sex. Once, his boss had asked him a round-a-bout ques-tion meant to see if Harvey was straight. Harvey, incredulous, had asked him, "Why would you want beef jerky when you could have prime rib?!" All the guys in his crew considered themselves lucky to have such a dedicated coach. Sure he was hard on them, sometimes incredibly hard, but he had mustered a team that was the best rigging team in the business - and they all knew it.

"Harvey, this is the third time in as many months that you've fired the gauge controller, what gives?" Burton Barnsworth, Harvey's regional director, was on the rig for the week, checking the crew's production, safety measures, and the rig's overall profitability.

Harvey had never liked Burton. Burton had just started with the company six months ago. Burton talked with a nasal tone and was almost always condescending. He had never worked on a rig, had no idea what it was like to command a team of men to peak performance, and had been given his position by his uncle (half-owner of Goldman Oil) in the corporate office. He had inherited his father's fortune (the other half-owner) and thought that going around to the oil rigs to familiarize himself with the business was "the right thing to do." What had exasperated Harvey even more on this particular visit from Burton was that he had brought his wife with him. Burton had brought her because they were going to vacation for a few weeks in a beach house on the mainland after his week's "job" was over. Bunny (Harvey could never believe that could be her real name) was quite the sideshow. She wore two or three different outfits, every day, complete with matching wide-brimmed sun hats. She and her poodle used the upper deck to jog around in the mornings. If Harvey heard Burton call her "Bunny" one more time, he had promised himself he would immediately throw them both overboard. Now, Burton was complaining how Harvey was handling his job.

"Well, if the suits in human resources wouldn't keep sending me these boys from the local surf club, maybe I wouldn't have to keep sending 'em back home. You take care of your job and I'll take care of mine."

"Well, hang on now, Harvey; don't bite the hand that feeds you. I was just coming out to propose a celebration to you for all the help you've given me and the hard work you've done these past couple of weeks while I've been here. My Bunny and I wish to take you and a guest of your choice to the Oceanside tomorrow night - what do you say?"

My Bunny....my Bunny, wait......food. "Uh, anything we want on the menu?"

"Uh, yeah, anything!"

"Any guest?"

"Sure, you bring any young filly you want to impress."

"Well, actually, Bortz has been a great hand for me on the rig and I've been needing to give him a pat on the back for some time. This'll be the perfect way to do it. Hey Bortz, you're dining with me at the Oceanside tomorrow night, courtesy of Goldman!"

"You kidd'n me, boss? They tell me it's a Ben Franklin to eat there. I'd have to see if my polyester suit still fits."

"Nobody deserves it better than you, Bortz; you're the type of guy that makes this company great. Without you, how could Burton and Bunny

afford their stylish but very important lifestyle?"
He shot a grin toward Burton.

Chapter Three

Sheila was having a rough day. Chance's father, Stewart, had just dropped by her apartment and back into her life. She remembered the summer she went to the beach with her parents in another lifetime and being smashed by a larger-than-life wave. She had been overpowered and dragged under. When she finally got to her feet, she was coughing seawater and sand out of her mouth, and picking sand out of her ears and nose. She felt a little like that now. Stewart wanted to get back together again, now that he knew that Chance was not given much longer to live. Sheila had told him out of duty about Chance's condition – since he was the boy's father. Now, Stewart figured that once Chance was gone, he and Sheila could resume their relationship again. Just seeing him through her apartment security peephole had made her blood boil. She had let him in out of sheer curiosity for his boldness to hunt her down. She had thought that maybe he had come to see

Chance. Or, at least maybe he had come with some money to help with Chance's survival. He wasted no time in making his intentions known to Sheila that when Chance was gone he wanted to start up their relationship again. Sheila had let her intentions be known to Stewart with her favorite blue glass vase crashing against his skull as he quickly exited her apartment. *Jefferson had it right, all men are created equal: a bunch of idiot vermin.*

To make matters worse, Tom had witnessed the ending of her meeting with Stewart. He was visiting with a parishioner two doors down and was leaving at the same time as Stewart's hasty exit. Stewart careened off of Tom and grasped at the back of his bloody head as he left.

"You've got to work on your customer service!" Tom quipped. She knew by his grimace that he realized the split-second after his line that it wasn't humorous.

Not caring, she spat, "I've got a couple of vases left, and as you can tell, I'm pretty accurate at throwing them, preacher."

"Now, don't be hasty. Bad joke. If it's any consolation, you were my next stop."

"Are you getting lonely, married to the church, or are you going to try to convert me?" Sheila asked sarcastically. "I'm too expensive for you if you came for pleasure, and I don't have the time if you came to tell me I'm going to hell."

"Touché, touché, Sheila. Would you go to dinner with me tomorrow night?" asked Tom.

"Go to dinner with you?!" Sheila couldn't think of a more uncomfortable thing to do, let alone all the business she would lose.

"Yes, and you'll be well compensated for it," he explained.

"You certainly are a different kind of priest," said Sheila, uncertainly.

"Come on, I'll pick you up at seven here tomorrow."

"Alright, but you better make it worth my while, preacher, I've got some important bills to get paid."

"I think you'll be pleasantly surprised, Sheila," said Tom, with a slight grin on his face. And, before she could change her mind, he quickly went down the steps and got into his car.

As Sheila went back into her apartment, she heard her phone ringing. Her caller i.d. said, " Miami Children's Hospital."

Dear God, don't let it be bad news about Chance. "Hello, this is Sheila."

"Sheila, this is Dr. Bryant's office. I need to speak with you about the financial arrangements for the treatment for Chance, can you come in tomorrow?" The office manager for Dr. Bryant, Myra, had been very leery of setting up the treatments for Chance. Myra could sense that the funding for the potentially life-saving medication was in question from the start, and Sheila knew it. She had looked into Sheila's eyes, as she had hundreds of clients before, and could sense Sheila was lying about "the money coming from her aunt in a week."

"Myra, I'm working tomorrow, can't you tell me now what you want?" Sheila asked in frustration.

"I would rather have talked with you in person, but if you can't come in, I suppose this will have to do," Myra said.

"Spit it out, it can't make this day any worse," Sheila said wryly.

"It's about the financial arrangements for Chance's treatment," she said in uncharacteristic meekness. "You said your aunt was supposed to have given you the last twenty-five thousand by Monday. Sheila, we can't start treatments with Chance until we've received final payment. In order to give him this chance at life with this program, we have got to have this last payment by Friday - only two days from now, do you understand?"

"Do you have children, Myra?"

"I understand how you feel, Sheila, but there's noth..."

"I know there's not a damn thing you can do about it, Myra, but don't you *ever* tell me you understand how I feel unless your only child, the only ray of sunshine in your life, is laying life-less in a hospital with a few months to live. But by God, if it takes the last breath I breathe to get you this last twenty-five thousand dollars to give Chance this hope of life, I'll do it. You'll have your money by Friday, Myra." Sheila slammed down the receiver.

The weight of the last few months was unbearable for Sheila. The only reason she hadn't tried ending her life a dozen times was her mission to give Chance every shot to live. As she sobbed into both hands, she remembered how Chance used to be. He was such a vibrant little boy. A favorite memory of Sheila's was how Chance always wanted to help her with putting the dishes away. After dinner, he would say he wanted to "help Momma." Sheila always let him and tried to train him to not be scared of doing kitchen work. He had broken several dishes and glasses, but Sheila hadn't cared, he was her little man.

Another memory that always tugged at her heart was the day Chance brought home a stray cat. The neighbor boys were trying to mistreat it by throwing rocks at it and had broken one of its legs. Chance had grabbed it, saving it from the torture, and brought it home. Of course, Sheila and Chance had tied an ice cream stick to its leg and nursed it back to health. They had named him Rocky because of what the cat had been saved from.

They did everything together, until the day Chance finally had to be hospitalized. Sheila had quit her job to be with him in the hospital, reading, playing games, and just talking with him. The doctors had said that there wasn't much they could do for Chance - and that he would slowly deteriorate. Then, Dr. Bryant had told Sheila about an experimental treatment that had worked in some cases for some people, especially children. It was a gamble against the odds, but if Sheila could get the money together, he would be willing to try it. That was the very day that Sheila had gotten in touch with some unsavory characters from her ex-boyfriend's past. "Sure, we're always looking to expand our business," they had said, looking hungrily at her tall frame, long legs, and well-built figure. "In fact, we'll even be your first paying customers."

Her nosedive into prostitution had taken its toll on her, but she always carried a picture of Chance with her to lift her spirits and remind herself of her mission. Her split of the money had been much more than she could've earned any-where else with a high school education, but she was still twenty-five thousand short.

Alright, I've got to get it together; I've only got two days left. Even though Sheila knew it was almost impossible to raise that kind of money in such a short period of time, she dried her face, blew her nose and, exhausted, walked out the door to give it her best shot. *Dear God, if You're really out there, help me save my baby boy.*

Chapter Four

Burton and Bunny picked up Harvey and Bortz in a stretch limo at Harvey's place. Harvey had gotten a great deal on a "fixer upper" a block off the ocean. He hadn't realized how much fixing the small bungalow would need at the point of sale, but he figured that he had the rest of his life to work on it between his shifts at Goldman. He loved it here: the hot weather, the sand, the smell of the ocean, the sound of the seagulls. When he and Bortz had graduated high school in a small town in Michigan, they had celebrated by coming here for a month. They fell in love with the atmosphere of the laid back beach life. When Goldman Oil had run an advertisement hiring riggers, they knew they had to try out for the positions. Hired on the spot, they were living their dream. Bortz had married a few years later, but Harvey hadn't "settled down" yet.

"Look, Bunny, look at the beautiful sunset," Burton was saying.

"Oh, it's so fabulous, honey," replied Bunny

"Harvey and Bortz, isn't this the life, cruising down the ocean in a limo towards one of the finest restaurants in the state?" preened Burton.

"It's a great treat, Burton, but nothing compares to having a few friends over for a cookout on the beach," Harvey said, with Bortz nodding in agreement.

"You can't tell me that you always want to live life in the same... well... part of town do you?" pried Burton.

"To be honest with you, boss, I'm livin' my own 'la vida loca.' I've got a steady, well payin' job, the respect of my peers, great friends, and time for a little fun. I've heard it doesn't get much better than that. If I had a big house, fancy car, and large bank account, I'd always be worried about how to take care of everything. To me, there's a lot more to get out of life than chaining yourself down to a bunch of stuff," reasoned Harvey.

"Speak for yourself, Harvey," chimed in Bortz, "I need one of those new sixty-five-inch 3-D plasma television sets, I wouldn't mind taking care of that baby. I'd dust it every morning, and kiss it every night."

Everyone had a good laugh.

Bortz was Harvey's right hand man. When Harvey was quarterback and captain of the football team his senior year, he made sure everyone knew who was second in command. Bortz was on the heavy side, but strong as an ox. He was a linebacker for Harvey and very rarely ever let anyone through to lay a hand on him.

They had been great friends ever since the day that their fifth grade class was on recess during a cold snowy day in late winter. Bortz was getting roughed up by the class bully, Barry. Barry was trying to make a show of him because he had refused to make an inferior baseball card trade. This was bad for Barry's future baseball card trading business. So Barry, who had already flunked two grades (and was failing fifth grade) had Bortz in a head lock, trying to twist off his neck. Harvey noticed that the big kid was picking on the smaller one. Knowing that he could easily be the victim next time, he took a rock the size of a golf ball and zinged it as hard as he could at Barry's head. Harvey had always been good at throwing baseballs, dodge balls, whiffle balls, *any* kind of ball, and, yes, rocks as well. Needless to say, Barry cried out in pain and let Bortz go. Then, they both rushed him and knocked him flat. With blood oozing from his rock wound, they told him that if he ever touched anyone in class again that year, there would be a lot more coming to Barry. Harvey was pretty sure he had seen their teacher look the other way while they gave Barry what was coming to him. Barry seemed to be less aggressive with his classmates after that. With Harvey's throwing ability and Bortz's tackling skills, they formed a great friendship that day that not only served them well all through their high school football years, but gave them a bond that only a small percentage of people ever enjoyed."The only thing I could chain myself to, and kiss goodnight, would be something of the feminine variety," said Harvey thoughtfully. "Not some little creature that needs everything done for her or a gal that cries when she breaks a nail. But, someone that wants to live life right alongside of me."

"I suppose you'd love it if she could belch her ABC's, too," Bunny said, bristling.

"Now, that's my kind of woman!" piped in Bortz.

Bortz's wife, Sadie, could hold her own around the table when Harvey was over and Bortz declared a belch-off after a few drinks. She won her share of first prizes. She was not one for "lily white boys" as she called them, and her Bortz was far from it at six feet five and two hundred eighty pounds.

"I'll definitely take my love kitten, Bunny, over any of the baser sort," replied Burton. "I also think that given the chance, you two would swap lifestyles with me in a heart-beat. The fine wine, chauffeurs, exotic vacations, tailored suits, the personal chef, the mansions, I could go on and on. I wouldn't trade my position for anything in the world. I suppose I'm addicted to it. But what a thing to be addicted to! I love everything about my life, and there's nothing too big or costly to bestow on my little Bunny Barnsworth." Burton's speech ended with Bunny and Burton rubbing noses.

If it wasn't for this meal, I would be jumping from this moving limo right about now, thought

Harvey. "Driver, aren't we about there yet?" he asked anxiously.

Chapter Five

Sheila had been out all night and all the next morning. She had never "worked" so hard in all her life. She was in "sales," and sell herself she did. Her take home pay was the best she'd had of her new career. However, she was far short of the amount she needed to turn in tomorrow. She still needed nineteen thousand dollars and time was almost gone. Her hopes were resting on her time with Tom tonight. She fell fast asleep until time for her "date" with the priest.

Tom showed up at ten till seven. He was taken aback when Sheila came to the door in a simple black knee-length dress - not anything like he'd seen her wear before. Her hair was up and her make-up was not intended to draw attention from a block down the street. In short, she looked very elegant.

"You look uh...well...different, I mean nice tonight," bungled the priest.

"I thought about skipping your offer of dinner many times, Father Tom," replied Sheila, "because something I've been busy working on isn't finished yet. I really shouldn't take the time to go out with you tonight, but you're my last hope to reach my goal."

"I thought I told you that you can call me Tom. What is your goal?"

"I...I can't get into that right now, I'll tell you tonight. I do appreciate the help you've given me in the past."

"I've been glad to, Sheila. I'd like to see you rise above your current circumstances. Everyone deserves a helping hand who is willing to accept one."

"God knows, if there ever was a time when I needed help, this one would qualify," replied Sheila. "There's something I need to know, though."

"Sure, what is it?"

"Are you going to need anything else from me tonight besides dinner? I mean, it's okay if you do; your money is just as good as another's. It's just that I'd like to know up front."

"You're asking me if I need sex tonight? No, no, I gave up on that pleasure ten years ago when I donned this collar. You are a beautiful woman, but I have a much more pure interest in you, Sheila. I hope I can help you reach your goal."

For some reason, this put Sheila more at ease with him. "We'll see if you can, Tom."

....

Tom and Sheila walked toward his car, which was a regular in the neighborhood. A teenage boy smoking a cigarette in the shadows of a nearby alley spotted the priest and Sheila getting in the priest's car. "Hey, preacher, you gone from bangin' pulpits to prettier things now?"

"Don't let that punk kid bother you," said Sheila.

"If I let what people think about me affect me, I would have quit a long time ago," replied Tom.

The priest was telling the truth to Sheila. There wasn't much that he had not already been through, either before he became a priest or after the fact. He had grown up in a rough neighborhood in Miami. He had been a member of a gang, the Knights, for a few years with Nick, his older brother. One day the gang broke into a jewelry store to see what they could get. It was two a.m. and no one would have thought that the owner was asleep in the back. It turned ugly with a shootout between the owner and two members of the Knights. Two people died: the owner and Tom's older brother. Seeing his brother lying there in a pool of blood with a bullet hole in his head, Tom decided that was his last day in a gang.

His mother couldn't handle the loss. Tom's father and mother had divorced a few years earlier and it was very hard to raise two teenage boys in their neighborhood. Unable to escape the area because of her low-paying job, she blamed herself for Nick being in the situation he was in and his subsequent death. Her depression spiraled downward until one morning Tom couldn't wake his mother up. As he took her hand to check her pulse, an empty pill bottle fell out and onto the floor.

As Tom's life spiraled downward, he met a priest in the run-down parish a couple of blocks away. The guy was a big man at six-feet-four and every bit of two hundred thirty pounds. He had long hair down to his shoulders and his face was pock-marked and overly weathered for his forty-two years. He had been sent to this area because the other available candidates had picked "better" areas in which to live and minister. Once people met Father Mally, though, they were completely disarmed by his kindness and generosity. Even though he could pass for a Dodge City saloon bouncer, he was the type of guy people wanted to invite to their home to have baked lasagna and bounce their little ones on his knee.

The group Tom hung out with was antagonistic to him, however. Father Mally had been the overseer at the church for about six years, most of Tom's young adult life. One night, Tom and three other Knights had approached him about ten p.m. as Father Mally was going out to his car. There, in the dark, they had told him they needed all his money, or they were going to cut him up real good. Father Mally, calmer than Tom had seen anyone they had ever robbed, had said, "Sure, boys, but all you had to do was ask - no need to go to all this trouble." Reaching down into his wallet, he pulled out one hundred twenty dollars, showing them that was all that was there. "Before you go, I've got a little something extra to give you boys." He reached into his car and gave each of the Knights a small copy of the New Testament with some of the money just inside each front cover. He also mentioned that on Saturday nights, a group of teenagers from the neighborhood met at the parish to hang out, play sports, and eat. He invited the Knights to come. The older boys had cursed the priest, and told him if he ever tried to push religion on them again that they would kill him. Father Mally had seemed sad instead of scared of their threats. He told them if they ever needed someone to talk to, they knew where to find him. The meeting with Father Mally lodged in Tom's heart and memory. Tom figured the other three had probably thrown the books aside when they got home, to get at the money, but he had kept his and read out of it every once in a while.

The very morning of his mother's suicide, Tom walked out his door down the street toward the church to talk to Father Mally. Ethereally, Father Mally was standing in the middle of the street three blocks down, in front of the church, looking directly at him. Tom would never forget how he looked on that windy fall day. Trash was blowing all around past Tom and then on past the priest. The same wind that was pushing him toward Father Mally was gripping the priest's long black hair and throwing it back over his shoulders. The priest's black overcoat was getting ripped back the same way - like a jib sail broken free from its moorings. It seemed like there was no one else out on the street. Tom couldn't even hear anything else except for the rushing of the wind. *What is happening? Am I having some kind of psychedelic reaction, here?* The walk toward the priest was short, but seemed like it was in slow motion in Tom's mind. He thought about his parents' divorce and how his dad never came around anymore. He thought about his time with the Knights, the fighting, robberies, and all the stuff he'd been involved in. He thought about his brother's death and funeral and the heartbreak. And finally, he thought about his mother's lifeless body holding the empty pill bottle. It was too much. He had read enough of the book that the priest had given him to know what he was being pushed into. *God, this had better be what You say it's supposed to be, because I'm overly ready for the change. You've got one crazy-looking priest, but he looks exactly like what I need.*

Sobbing with the release of emotions, Tom came to the open arms of Father Mally. Nothing was said for what seemed like several moments until the priest said, "Tom, let's get you off the street." Then, he took him into the church.

Father Mally had been Tom's mentor from then on, helping him pass his GED, and get a job. Tom also helped out with the church's outreach to the kids in the neighborhood. He was often seen talking with a young boy on the verge of joining a gang or just spending too much time on the streets. One day, Tom realized that his work with the church was crowding out his time to do his "regular" job. He talked with Father Mally about becoming a priest. Father Mally couldn't hide his expanding chest, but told Tom to take a month and earnestly think about what he was thinking of doing. "Celibacy, modest pay, and living to serve others are some tough decisions that shouldn't be made in haste," he had told Tom. "However, should your choice still be yes, I don't think there would ever be a more qualified life to don this collar."

Tom had spent the month in great soul searching and was more than ready to take the plunge into priesthood. After he had completed the requirements of the Church, he had come back to Father Mally and his own old neighborhood to serve. Father Mally and Tom had helped many, many troubled kids get out of the gangs, addictions, and destructive mindsets that entrapped souls in terrible neighborhoods. Then, one day, Father Mally let Tom know that he would be leaving. He was being reassigned to an area near the Louisiana bayous. Tom knew he would be great for such a place, but would be sorely missed.

Now, Tom had been the main priest at the parish for seven years...

He was jolted from his thoughts by a female voice. "So, where are we going for dinner?"

"How does the Oceanside sound?" questioned Tom with a grin.

"The Oceanside! You must be joking. Are you sure you want to spend that kind of money on me?" asked Sheila.

"I can't think of a more worthy cause," replied the priest.

Chapter Six

Bortz, Harvey, Burton, and Bunny slid out of their limo and headed in to the Oceanside. It was tastefully decorated in exquisite furnishings with a coastal motif. As a customer walked in on the left side of the building, she was greeted by staff, her reservations were checked, and then she was led to her dining experience. A huge aquarium was also on the left, becoming the north end of the restaurant, with many kinds of sea life including sharks, sea bass, eels, and a man of war. There were six divers in the aquarium around a sea "set" consisting of a ten-foot clamshell with a built-in throne and several faux coral seats nearby. The male diver was dressed like Poseidon, with a scepter in one hand. The other five divers were females in mermaid costumes. Their air tanks were cleverly disguised in the back of their costumes. They were usually present in the evenings, putting on a show feeding the various sea creatures.

In the middle of the room, was a large area set up for entertaining guests. There was a pink twelve-foot-tall clamshell on a stage that could rotate three hundred sixty degrees. Several microphone stands were bolted in place in front of the large clamshell. Straight ahead, glass windows from floor to ceiling enabled the viewer to see a gorgeous view of the veranda, beach, and ocean. On the right, two sets of double doors led to the kitchen area.

An Oceanside diner could sit and enjoy the fine dining experience from three vantage points. One could dine outside on the beach by candlelight, on the veranda overlooking the ocean, or inside the establishment with a view of the sea life nearby in the aquarium.

The Oceanside was the hot spot for the upper class crowd. It was always packed out and people had to reserve a table at least a month in advance. They could go on standby and pay an extra fifty dollars per plate to get in if they didn't have reservations. Every night, several young gentlemen, in hopes of impressing their date for the evening, would be waiting to see if there would be any standby tables available. Every once in a while, there would be a vacancy, but more times than not, they were turned away with the short reply of, "Next time, you'll need to make a reservation."

After Burton confirmed their reservation, they followed their waitress to their table by the aquarium. The place was buzzing with conversation and the clinking of fine utensils. The Goldman

Oil team did not see another empty table as they were being ushered to their place. The food smelled so good, Harvey and Bortz looked at each other licking their lips with a knowing gaze and a groan.

Their waitress was dressed in a green sequined mermaid costume similar to the ones in the aquarium. The bottom part had separations for her legs, though, and the top was a simple green swimsuit. Her hair was as red as fire, as was the other ladies-of-the-sea-now-turned-waitresses. This redundancy could have been a boring mistake from the management, but inasmuch as Harvey could tell, the ladies who had been hired as wait-resses could have come straight from Poseidon's harem. Each one was uniquely breathtaking.

As they walked past a group having their order taken, they noticed that the waiter had the same Poseidon costume as the diver in the aquarium. Just as the waitresses had been picked for their attractiveness, the waiters were not the average high school geeks. "Good grief, look at the size of that guy's biceps," remarked Bortz as they walked past. He was of similar stature as the other waiters that Bortz could see around the room: deep tan, rippled stomach, and tree trunk legs. There were two qualifications for a male that waited tables at the Oceanside, Bortz surmised. First, he had to be a body builder by day, to work here by night. Second, he had to have a hairy, muscled chest to look real good in the low-cut Poseidon outfit.

"Isn't this place a hoot?" Burton exclaimed, as he slapped Harvey on the back.

The attendants seemed to come out of thin air to be of service to the group. Chairs were pulled back, napkins placed in laps, and drinks were poured.

"I'm definitely impressed, Burton - great pick of restaurants. If the food is as good as the atmosphere, I'll be in heaven," replied Harvey.

"I fear I'm in danger of being banished to Hades since I can't quit looking at that waiter over there," joked Bunny.

"Maybe this will help, my little she-devil," said Burton placing an open menu in front of Bunny's face. "This will tempt you in a more pure way."

The menus were large faux clamshells made from resin with a hinge in the middle and a clasp on the outside for securing them when not in use. When the clamshell opened, the appetizers and drinks were on the left and the main courses and desserts were on the right. The colors of the menu added ambience to the restaurant. The waitresses made sure that the pastels of pink, sea green, amber, and sky blue were staggered so that no table of four had two of the same color.

They were positioned in one of the best tables inside the restaurant. Bortz was fascinated by a shark that was swimming within a foot of him. *He looks as hungry as I am.* He had to tap a few times on the eighteen-inch thick see-through glass to give himself a little more confidence that he couldn't be dinner.

Chapter Seven

It was seven-thirty by the time Tom and Sheila were seated at their table on the beach. The waves of the ocean were rolling in about six feet from their chairs. The sunset was especially spectacular this evening with a reddish-orange glow originating from the west and diminishing fainter and fainter to a slight pink toward the east. The wavy pattern of the clouds being kissed by the rays from the sun's decline gave the appearance of a second reddish ocean in the sky. The candle burning between them provided a pleasing amount of light and a rose scent that added to the peaceful surroundings. Even the beach had been raked into three-inch furrows resembling soft earth waves. The two unlikely dinner companions listened to the soothing sounds of the waves and took in the visual feast without talking for a few moments after they were seated.

The priest was the first to speak. "I now see why this is the most popular spot in town. What do you think, Sheila?"

"I think that this is all a dream. This is by far the best I've ever been treated by anyone, especially a man," she said with a mist in her eyes. Then, she looked away. "But, I'd be lying if I told you my heart wasn't breaking as I'm experiencing this heavenly scene."

"I've got a confession to make, Sheila," said Tom. "Ever since I first saw you on the streets, I made it my business to find out about you. There was something different in your attitude that compelled me to meet you. It is as if you have a purpose for living that others in your profession do not possess. One night I followed you to see where you lived. Then, I inquired about you in your apartment building, where some of the members of our parish also live. It just so happens that Molly Baird resides two doors down from you. I was visiting her the other night when I... you uh... told me about your vase collection."

"Well, Tom!" Sheila's eyes were flashing. "I can't figure you out. One minute I think you're the only man left on the earth worth getting to know and the next minute I'm wondering if you're a stalker that's going to try to slice me up and bury me under the floor boards!" She slapped her purse flat on the table, getting ready to stand to leave.

Sheila had confided in Molly one night about Chance when both were out on their small verandas, getting some fresh air. Molly had once had a six-year-old girl, but lost her when she was killed on the sidewalk by a hit-and-run driver. The women had talked several times together. Sheila considered Molly her only friend in the neighborhood.

Isn't anything sacred anymore? Sheila wondered.

"Hold on now, Sheila, let me finish," said the priest urgently. "I was getting ready to tell you that Molly wouldn't tell me anything about you at first. She was afraid it would betray your friendship. But, I implored her to tell me because I had a hunch I could help you. She only told me about Chance and his condition after I assured her that I would do everything in my power to help you get off the streets. You can't blame her for being a good friend, Sheila. Again, please, call me Tom."

"A few other things come to my mind to call you, Tom," said Sheila with her eyes softening again. "So, that was why you gave me the money a few weeks ago."

"I would have given you more, but I hadn't seen you around lately," said Tom.

Sheila paused. She could see that Tom was probably not a serial killer that had been hunting her. Her mood turned melancholy again. "I have to have my final payment in tomorrow to pay for a last chance treatment for my son. I've been busy trying to raise the money for it the only way I could," she whispered, looking down ashamedly with large teardrops welling in her eyes.

"Well, I don't know how much you have left to raise, but you can count on me and the parish to be one of your donors," said Tom handing her a large stuffed envelope.

Sheila's face broke out into a big smile. "Is this what I think it is?"

"Open it up and see," replied Tom, adjusting his collar.

Sheila quickly tore out the side of the envelope and slid out a huge wad of cash. Tears welled up in her eyes again, this time with gratefulness. She quietly thanked the priest, stood up, went to him and gave him a hug for a few seconds. Tom had long ago stopped worrying about what other people thought of him, but he smiled as they hugged, because he knew what this must look like to the raised eyebrows of their fellow Oceanside diners. Usually it wasn't a good scenario with a very pretty woman, a priest and two fistfuls of cash changing hands, but Tom wasn't a conventional operator. The members of his church had told him that more times than he could remember. He was sure his fellow diners would go home with a spicy tale to tell.

"Thanks, again, Tom," said Sheila as they both sat back down.

"There's about five thousand there," mentioned Tom as he sat down as well.

Sheila's eyes were turning sad again. "This is a mixed blessing. Don't get me wrong, I'm very appreciative of the money, but it looks like I'm still going to be fourteen thousand short, so you may as well not waste the church's money on me." She put the money back in the envelope and pushed it back across the table toward Tom. "I'll always be grateful for your generosity."

"That's your money, Sheila. You do what you need to do with it. You never know what God is going to do. Nothing is ever too late if it's something that is on His schedule."

"Well, if he ..... If he doesn't make it through this, at least I'll have something for his f...f... funeral," Sheila broke down for a few seconds and had to gather herself. Tom gave her his monogrammed hanky to use. He wasn't the hanky carrying type, but he had received it as a present last Christmas from a couple in his church. They were going to get a divorce, but through several months of Tom's counseling, decided to love each other again. Carrying it brought him the warm feeling that miracles happened every day, but sometimes they required grit and determination.

Seconds later a waiter came by (muscles and all) with a tissue box, and asked Sheila if everything was all right. He eyed the priest warily as if he was the culprit of her distress. Tom was eyeing his massive frame and wondering how much money Oceanside must be paying their employees to get such impressive specimens. He had already chided himself for visiting a little too much with the mermaid that had checked their reservations.

It wasn't just the sparkling sequins adorning the sea creature's dress that had mesmerized the priest momentarily. Being married to the Church definitely had its times of chafing and Tom was not immune.

The waiter, noticing that Sheila had calmed herself, left the two alone again. "I'll get you two your menus," he said as he trudged back shoeless through the sand.

Sheila sniffed a few more times and pulled herself completely back together. She had hardly ever cried growing up and she had not under-stood why most of her female counterparts were so emotional. Lately, though, the tears had come frequently. "I'm so sorry that you had to witness this, Tom. I used to be such a strong person, but recently I've had a lot on my mind, I guess." She finished wiping the corners of her eyes and put the hanky in her purse. "Thank you for the hanky; I'll wash it and get it back to you."

"That's fine, you can give it back to me when ..." His voice was drowned out by an urgent Middle East-accented voice yelling over the restaurant's public address system:

"EVERYONE MOVE IMMEDIATELY TO THE MIDDLE OF THE MAIN BUILDING. FAILURE TO DO SO WILL RESULT IN YOUR QUICK DEMISE!!!

PART 2

Chapter Eight

Everyone in the restaurant, on the veranda, and on the beach sat in stunned silence for a few seconds. The Goldman group had just finished eating their appetizers of stuffed crab, fresh jumbo shrimp, and lobster tails. The place had been hopping with gaiety a moment before. Now, not a breath was heard.

Bortz cut the silence momentarily. "Maybe this is some Gucci-wearing, fancy pants' idea of a joke, but I..."

Deafening machine gun and pistol fire exploded from uncountable positions around the restaurant and out back. Everyone slammed as hard as they could down onto the floor to keep from being hit.

Outside, on the beach, the terrified customers, including Tom and Sheila, were lying face down on the sand, trying to get as low as possible. Men in suits and tuxedos along with women in their best formal evening wear, jewelry, and hairdos were not concerned with getting sandy at the moment.

"I SAID TO MOVE TO THE CENTER OF THE MAIN BUILDING, NOW!" came the loud, screaming voice over the intercom again.

This time everyone immediately stood up and bolted toward the center of the restaurant.

Harvey, Bortz, Burton, and Bunny quickly stood up as well to comply with the stern command. Pieces of sheet-rock and debris were still dropping from the ceiling all over the room where the ammunition had been fired. Overhead lights were flickering or demolished and dust permeated the place. People started coughing. As Harvey was walking toward the center of the building, he noticed that a couple of the servers were separated from the customers. He caught sight of a waiter and waitress surrounding the group along with five well-dressed men with Middle Eastern features. They were carrying the guns that had just rocked the place. The men in suits and the rippled Poseidon look-a-like were carrying the machine guns, and the mermaid was sporting a forty-five caliber Rutger. All the other waiters and waitresses were in the same unfortunate situation as him, it seemed, as he scanned the crowd.

The closest gunman to Harvey was about five feet away, to his left, with his back to the aquarium. Harvey glanced his way and saw that the tip of his Poseidon's scepter was slid back. Protruding from its end was a machine gun barrel. He was yelling something in Arabic and motioning menacingly with the gun to the Goldman group. They didn't need the services of a translator to understand they were to keep moving forward toward the center of the room. The mermaid was standing at the entrance to the Oceanside just to Harvey's right. The side of her outfit along her right thigh was unzipped and Harvey immediately knew how the mermaid was able to hide her pistol.

One unique thing about the sea creatures gone bad was their skin color. As far as Harvey could tell, they were probably from the same part of the world as their suited counterparts. *Oh hell, we've stepped into some kind of terrorist action.*

Since Sheila and Tom were the farthest away from the main building, they were the last ones inside, behind the veranda customers, and the others that were seated in the beach area. The waiter that had helped Sheila with the tissues was being herded right in front of her. As the priest, who was bringing up the rear, climbed the steps past an armed suit onto the veranda, the gunman slammed the butt of his weapon into Tom's lower back, near his right kidney, and yelled something in Arabic. The priest crumpled to the ground just inside the restaurant in agony.

....

Tom had felt some serious physical pain before in his youth. He had gotten into several all-out gang fights over turf in Miami and had broken quite a few bones and sported several scars to show for it. But, he had also given his share of pain and suffering as well. When he had been with the Knights for only three months, they were ambushed during a group meeting in an abandoned warehouse around midnight. His brother was suffering from a horrible stomach virus and was at home throwing up everything he had eaten the past few days and a few things he didn't think he had eaten. Tom was nervous to be there without him, but he was also determined to not live in his brother's shadow.

A tough young kid, Martinez, from one of their rivals, the Killers, had joined the Knights the day before. As he put it, "I just wasn't gettin' enough respect from those fools." He wanted to start a new career with the Knights, and the Knights were more than happy to oblige. They had even given him a spot among the twelve "counselors." These twelve counselors advised the Knights' president. They knew it would mean a vicious rumble with the Killers, but hey, they didn't join a gang to sit in a coffee house drinking lattes. Besides, the inner gratification of receiving the defection from their rival was worth a thousand gang wars.

Tom had been sitting closest to the door when it was bashed in. He received an immediate concussion from a blow to the head with a metal pipe. His only contribution to the situation had been his startled expression that amused his assailant as he was conked.

The gangs of Miami, during this time, had called a truce declaring any type of gun off-limits during a gang war. Not that any of the leaders had gotten queasy about "gun violence." It was just that it was more satisfying, they felt, to fight mano a mano, where they could bang, punch, kick, stab, twist, cut, and gauge their enemy up close and personal. This Edict of Honor, as it was called, was followed for three years until someone snuck in a pistol to a gang fight and killed three rivals. He was terminated with an accurate throw to the jugular with a six-inch butcher knife, but nonetheless, no one trusted the Edict of Honor from then on and it was back to the more clinical "pop 'em from afar" mentality.

Tom must've been out for a few minutes. When he came to, he was witnessing one of the most vicious fights in which he had been involved. At least ten bloody guys were lying on the ground in various positions, moaning, worthless to rejoin their team. The new guy, Martinez, was proving his worth. He had pulled a machete from under his overcoat and was hacking his way through the jungle of a few of his old "disrespectful" cronies. Tom regained enough composure to return the surprise his pipe wielding foe had given him. He was just getting ready to smash the fat skull of a Knight, who had just fallen to his knees in agony from a sneaky below-the-belt kick by a skinny, long-haired Killer. Both hands were high above his head with a death grip on his trusty steel pipe ready to come down on his target's meaty head. He had the slight grin of a professional woodsman about to make kindling out of a dry old log. Tom enjoyed his victim's new facial expression when he broke three of his ribs with the metal chair in which he had been sitting. About that time, sirens were heard, coming fast. Both sides immediately dragged, carried, and pulled their wounded into dark alleys and soon vanished; leaving the police to rightly speculate that a bloody gang fight had taken place in the run-down warehouse.

Tom and Martinez were heralded as heroes from their peers. Tom was too young to be in the inner circle of counselors, but no one looked at him as Nick's younger brother from then on. The pain in his fractured skull lasted for nearly two months, but Tom couldn't have felt any better if he'd received the Medal of Honor.

Tom had many other skirmishes that, when looked back upon, he wondered how he had kept alive when so many others hadn't. He had been stabbed three times, in the chest twice and the back once; had been shot in the thigh, broken his right hand, and been punched and kicked countless times. He had been taken to the hospital seven times during the four years he was a Knight. His mother reminded him of this statistic constantly when she was alive.

....

How come I am always the one getting blindsided? Tom was on the ground in excruciating pain, grasping at his lower right back. *Oh, I haven't felt this much pain in years*. This was supposed to have been a relaxing evening by the ocean, giving a little hope to a woman in a heart-rending situation. Instead, this had all the makings of a brewing storm that was going to turn incalculably ugly. He looked up in time to see Sheila unthinkingly going into action. He didn't even have time to tell her to stop.

Chapter Nine

Sheila had a knack for bad relationships. On her first date, at the age of sixteen, she was date raped at a party. She didn't fare any better with her next choice. The relationship lasted for a whole year, but that was not something to be proud of. Ray was a good-looking nineteen-year-old who had just graduated high school the year before. He worked in Dean's Mechanic Shop a few blocks from where she lived. Her old jalopy, which she had just purchased with the five hundred dollars she had managed to save from her waitressing job, was giving her trouble. She took the beast down to the shop and asked them to do their free exam.

Ray, the mechanic's assistant, immediately knew that whoever was towering above him as he slid from under the '56 Chevy he was working on needed his full attention. A young, un-chaperoned beauty in a short skirt and midriff shirt didn't come along too often at Dean's Mechanic

Shop. In fact, as he thought about it, it never had happened before. Ray took full advantage of his opportunity. He worked hard to be the nicest guy she had met. He fixed her car for ninety-five dollars, even though he wrestled with the thing for two days straight. Even then, it was barely hobbled together enough to last a few months. That was all the time Ray needed. Sheila would come by after work and the two started getting serious. Before long, Sheila moved into his meager apartment, assuring her aunt and uncle that she was in love.

It wasn't very long before Sheila noticed a change in Ray. He was losing his temper with her in disagreements. She had thought he was a just a little more opinionated than most when they were getting to know each other. Now, she was getting a little worried she had made a mistake.

Ray went from bad to worse. He started smacking her around when she did something to displease him. It didn't help that he had started drinking more than usual. Sheila felt trapped. She didn't want to face the fact that she had chosen another loser. She had too much pride to let her aunt and uncle know that she had made a mistake and ask to move back in with them. Besides, she was dealing with just a few bruises and she was used to dealing with pain. Who knows, maybe she could get Ray to change and they could still live a wonderful life together.

That thought was blasted out of Sheila about a year into their relationship. Ray had just lost his job at the shop because he had shown up for the third time drunk. This was the last straw for his boss, who had been getting tired of dealing with Ray. He was fired on the spot and told to "get his ass off the property." The boss was a big man and Ray went looking for someone else on whom to take out his misfortune.

Sheila fit the bill. She was getting ready for work and had just finished fixing up for the early lunch crowd. She knew she was in trouble when she saw Ray stumbling up the front steps. He hadn't come home last night, and in the past that had meant that he'd been out with a few loser buddies drinking all night long. Sometimes he would knock Sheila around in these situations, and sometimes he'd fall on the couch and sleep all afternoon. He was usually awake and sober when she would get home around eight o'clock, and he would always apologize and say how pretty she was and that he would never do something like that again.

Sick of the same old routine, she tried to lock the door before he could get to the handle. Too late. He was in a drunken rage and someone had to pay for the darkness in his soul. He grabbed her and shoved her against the wall, knocking off the only photo of her parents that she had. It shattered along with her heart and body. Before Ray was done, he had broken her nose and arm, and had tried to strangle her. Just when she was becoming dizzy from the oxygen deprivation, she survived by grabbing his groin with her good arm and hand

and twisted with all her strength. His lethal hands quickly released her, and she lunged for the door. While Ray was contemplating whether his genitals were in the right spot or even still attached, Sheila was racing her old jalopy to the hospital to figure out the damage.

Still too proud and ashamed to report to the police, or anyone else for that matter, what was done to her, she told everyone that she had been in a car accident. She traded in her car for a slightly better one the day she was released from the hospital and no one knew the difference. Her relatives took her back in "just until I'm done recuperating," Sheila had told them. Unable to go back to work, she collected unemployment, hating every minute of it. While she was recuperating over the next few months, she had plenty of time to think about what went wrong. One thing was for certain, she would never let someone treat her that way again. As soon as she was fully recovered, she started a new job in a clothing manufacturing plant, rented a cheap apartment and enrolled in the Ti Lin School of Karate.

Ti was a patient but stern teacher and she learned very quickly. With her real life experiences as motivation, she was driven to become Ti's best student. Day in, day out, she went to class, went to work, and went home to practice. It seemed like her three years of lessons flew by. She wished her mother could see her when she was presented with her black belt for all the intense work and effort it had taken. The confidence it had given her was even more invaluable.

....

Two major aspects of karate were to defend oneself and to defend others. Sheila jabbed a quick side-kick into the perpetrator's stomach. Her high heels added a much more damaging element to the punishment and resulted in his excruciating pain. The bearded man doubled over to the ground, trying to breathe. A single deafening gun blast went off within a foot of Sheila's right ear. Not knowing whether she'd been shot, she wheeled around and threw a back fist at her assailant. Her arm was grabbed, thrust downward and shoved behind her back in agony. She was pushed, arm still twisted behind her back, toward the nearby wall so hard her feet barely touched the ground. She smacked into the wall with such force that she barely hung onto consciousness. She was faintly aware of the feel of the cold barrel of a pistol in her left ear.

"You want to play around? Let's play," hissed the mermaid, violently bending Sheila's head back by her hair in a tight-fisted grip.

"Jazira, not yet! Let her go!" commanded the operational leader, motioning to her with his scepter rifle. "We've got to get ready and we don't have much time."

"Too bad, I was really going to enjoy this." The smile on her face belied the cold-blooded degree of evil to which her heart had stooped over her years of taking lives. She had been very successful at her profession. Whatever flicker of goodness she'd had as a young girl, had been replaced by the fires of hate and religion gone bad. She stroked Sheila's hair as she left and whispered, "Before this is over, you and I will play again."

....

From what Harvey could tell, all the waiters and waitresses, except for the waiter that had demanded he move forward and the waitress that had just accosted a tall lady just inside the back door, were victims like everyone else. Something very sinister evidently had been going on with the ownership of this restaurant, and now tonight's clientele had been dragged into some kind of horror. There were approximately sixty people standing now in the middle of the room in a clearing where the best local talent had often crooned for the enjoyment of the Oceanside's customers.

The waiter that had been in front of Sheila helped Tom and Sheila over to the crowd at the center of the room. No one moved or spoke, for fear that their captors would think someone needed disciplining. They had all witnessed Sheila's correction. The only sounds were a muffled cough here and there. They waited for a seemingly long time, but an octopus-shaped clock above the back windows told Tom that it had been only three minutes until the reason they were all involved in this madness appeared.

Chapter Ten

A well-tanned Caucasian with black hair and blue eyes in his middle forties threw open the kitchen's double swinging doors. He briskly came toward the crowd. He was dressed in an island-print shirt open at the neck, showing several large gold chains and a thicket of black chest hair. He had on baggy khakis and boat shoes to round out his benign attire. He was smiling large as he stepped up on the stage in front of the huge, now bullet-riddled, seashell and picked up the nearest microphone off the floor. It let out a short, deafening squeal.

"Welcome to my Oceanside Restaurant, ladies and gentlemen. The service tonight will be a little different than usual at this fine establishment. You see, we're trying something more exciting tonight. It's called hostage taking. We had to have something to bargain with the U.S. government in exchange for our safe passage to Iran. It seems that we've worn out our welcome and it's time to go home. The bad thing for you all is that we've learned your government is coming tonight to take us into custody. We're not going to let that happen. We've been bad boys and girls, and we wouldn't be treated kindly. So, we'd rather you fine customers be along for the ride. As they say, 'misery loves company.'"

"You all can call me Louie - Louie Fisher. Tonight will be a complicated effort that will require your complete obedience to our instructions. Let me be very clear, if anyone fails to adhere to our recommendations in the strictest sense, you will be eliminated from our plan."

No one there had to read between the lines to know what Louie meant. Most swallowed hard. Louie continued, "There are sixty-two of you here this evening. That is too many for us to effectively manage, so two-thirds of you are going to be set free, right now. Then the remaining lucky ones will get to have me as your companion for our little adventure....we will break you up into groups of about ten each." He stopped momentarily and his mouth broke into a wide grin again. "Wow, this feels like I'm the conductor of a television reality show! We could call this 'Survivor Oceanside' or God forbid, 'The Biggest Loser'! We could even call this, 'Who Wants to Be an Escaped Millionaire'?! I know I do!"

He was on a roll. Ever since he had intercepted a cell phone call early this morning that the FBI would be trying to take him and his team out tonight, he had been rehearsing his contingency escape plan over and over with his subordinates. He was wound up like an over-caffeinated graduate student sitting down for his final exam. Would all his training help him pass the test tonight? The studying was all over and what was going to happen was going to happen. It was freeing for him, really. He was either going to escape back to his adopted country of Iran or die with his team in a blaze of glory with twenty of his loyal customers. *No more worrying, just a good 'ole fashioned machine gun battle with a few grenades and small rocket fire thrown in.*

Louie was not only a legend in his own mind, he was a legend with the Iranian government. He had been to Iran when he was a college student studying journalism. His final activity to graduate was to travel to a foreign country and interview twenty-five people about how they viewed their freedoms there. While most of his small class went to Mexico, Canada, or Europe for their final assignment, and a vacation, Louie had booked a plane for Saudi Arabia. After hiring an interpreter, he traveled across the Middle East to Iran and found an inexpensive motel close to a university to house the both of them for a couple of weeks. He had spent two weeks proudly getting his twenty-five interviews from his Iranian peers. He was very adept at setting people at ease with his disarmingly big smile. They had usually opened up to him when they were assured he didn't work for their government and false names would be used.

The day before he was to head back to the states, a young Iranian student, he had never met before, Sceva, knocked on his door and asked if he could talk with him about the U.S. After spending two weeks in Iran, Louie was glad to talk about something familiar to him for a change. After some small talk about what America was like, Sceva leaned toward Louie and announced in a low voice that he was sent with a proposition for Louie. It seemed that Louie had been carefully watched by government spies as he was illegally interviewing the university students. Louie was suddenly very nervous. Sceva assured him that instead of taking him into custody for a little discipline, Iranian-style; a better idea had been conceived. After seeing young Louie's courageousness to come to a totalitarian country and use his skills to get over twenty students to open up and speak frankly with him about their closed system of government, they wanted to see if he would work as a spy for a substantial amount of pay.

The plan was for Louie to graduate and obtain employment at a newspaper or television network. He would then send information to his contact about the schedules of various politicians, maps of important buildings, and any other information that they desired. His pay would be one million dollars per year, deposited in an untraceable off-shore account for his enjoyment. *Not bad for your first year out of college,* Louie thought. If he told anyone about the offer, they had people who could easily find him and end his life. If his answer was yes, then he would receive two hundred fifty thousand dollars in his new account before he arrived home, and two hundred fifty thousand per quarter from now on if his work was acceptable. Never having any patriotism, morals, or even much common sense, Louie said, "Yes," and was immediately a rich man.

He returned for his final few weeks of college, passing easily, and moved to the nation's capital, starting his career reporting with the *Washington D.C. Daily*. When asked how he could afford his lavish lifestyle, he told all of his colleagues that he had come from a wealthy family that still liked to dote on him. How else could he explain how he could afford his red customized Hummer and his sixty-five-hundred-square-foot brand-new home with pool and hot tub set on ten beautiful rolling acres just outside of town? All jealousies toward him were soon put aside, however. He threw at least one party a month at his humble abode for all his new friends. They were usually catered events with a talented local band cranking it up well into the wee hours of the morning.

In reality, his parents were far from rich. His dad, Clyde, had been sentenced to twenty-one years in jail for grand larceny and attempted murder. He had botched a bank robbery and ended up shooting an over-zealous young bank teller in the leg. The kid had become a local hero by tackling and de-masking Clyde as he tried to get away. The story of his debacle had always amused Louie.

Chapter Eleven

Louie had turned his back on his mother a long time ago. She could not afford the things Louie felt that he needed and she was always making rules that he couldn't live by. She also was always warning him he would turn out like his father if he didn't change his ways. He had enough of her seemingly endless over-protectiveness and moved out of the house his junior year in high school. He and an older buddy got an apartment together and Louie finished high school. Mrs. Fisher's heart was broken when her only child told her that he couldn't live in the same house with her anymore. But he knew his mother didn't understand what it took to make it big in this world. She had tried calling many times to talk, but he always had something he needed to get to and hung up. She even wrote him several times, but he never returned a single letter. There was so much for him to experience in life that he didn't need her trying to give him any advice.

Louie was with the *Washington D.C. Daily* for nine years building his reputation with the paper as well as with the Iranians. He developed some very good sources in Washington. He was able to relay to his "employers" many "off the record" conversations about American national security issues, schedules of politicians, diagrams of various important energy and water plants around the U.S. and much more. He knew he was the man they could count on to get them the information they needed. He would go to any length to do his job.

His work was the direct cause of a plane crash that killed a Republican lawmaker and his family. He was trying to rally support for bringing sanctions against Iran for sponsoring terrorists. The result of the investigation into the disaster was "engine failure." In reality, the night before the scheduled flight in the small craft, the engine had been sabotaged by two undercover Iranian terrorists. The flight schedule and whereabouts of the plane were easily obtained from Louie and transmitted to Sceva, his contact in Iran. The next day, the crash was front page headlines. He had received a private estate in Iran (confiscated from a successful businessman - but government enemy), a bonus of one million and a substantial raise. Now, his salary was two million per year.

Every once in a while his conscience would twinge at the thought of betraying the country that had given him his freedom. But just as quickly as those jitters would come, he thought about his lifestyle. What would life be like without his Hummer, mansion, or millions in his offshore bank account?

Some time in his tenth year in Washington D.C., he decided that he needed a better cover for all this money he was making. It was just too awkward to keep telling lies about his family continuing to send him money. He had made up so many stories about them, he was forgetting the dates and places and had started contradicting himself. Since his peers and co-workers were in the business of details, he was getting very nervous. At age thirty-two, he was also embarrassed that everyone thought he was living off his parent's money. A guy had to have some self-respect!

So, he located an expensive piece of real estate on the beach in an exclusive area of Miami and built the Oceanside. It was perfect! He could operate as a freelance journalist, still keep his old political contacts in Washington, make some new ones in Florida, have a large business in which to launder money, and be close to the coast to entertain arriving Iranian guests in the same non-traditional employment field as he.

The move to Miami worked out much better than Louie dreamed. He purchased a fifteen thousand-square-foot home on the ocean. He had been glad to get rid of the little place back in Washington. It had been cramping his style for several years. His new one had only been built three years ago and had been owned by an actor whose career had taken a turn for the worse and needed to liquidate some assets in a hurry. He had gotten a great deal. *My mother would be proud of my thriftiness*, Louie had thought, the day after his purchase, while sipping on a glass of wine by the near Olympic-sized pool.

He had a staff of live-in servants, all busy scurrying about trying to manage the palace. There were two drivers, a full-time master gardener, a personal chef (who had written three well-known national cook books), four maids to make everything shiny, a Spanish butler, two well-armed guards that complemented four viciously bred Dobermans, and a state-of-the-art security and fencing system that would allow only a military expedition to penetrate.

His new family of servants was getting paid an obscene amount more than their job status required. They, in return, were always offering a litany of daily compliments to Louie for how he dressed, what a great businessman he was with the Oceanside, and what an all-around great boss he was. His legendary status was becoming more and more obvious to him.

It was also becoming clear to a prominent Miami modeling agency. Louie had hired two Oceanside waitresses from Manuela's Modeling for a thousand dollars each per week on the spot. He met them while they were sunbathing on the beach near his estate. He had gone for a walk along the Atlantic to clear his head for a few minutes. He came upon the glistening bodies of two incredible specimens of bronzed female beauty.

Heather, blonde, and Molly, brunette, both long and lean, were on their stomachs, strapless, as he walked past. Knowing the magnetic charm he possessed, Louie moved in to dangle the bait. At first, the girls seemed annoyed that their conversation about Heather's new boyfriend was interrupted. However, Louie noticed that when their eyes travelled from his diamond studded Rolex to the three gold chains around his neck, they became interested in what he had to say. He knew that was why many girls sunbathed in this area of the beach; to see and be near the rich and famous. If they could actually meet someone of status here, then it meant an immediate elevation of stature in their social circle.

While sitting up, they tied their straps, and Louie thanked God he had moved from Washington to this change of climate where women could enjoy the warm weather unencumbered. He felt very warm himself, but not from the rising sun. He dabbed the beads of sweat from his forehead and began small talk. He found out that they were both about twenty-four and were hoping their modeling careers would take off. He lied and said he had some contacts in the industry and would be glad to put in some good words for them, if they wanted. They wanted. They especially wanted when they saw his estate rising from the palm tree-lined grounds as Louie humbly pointed to where he resided. Anyone living there must have contacts in all kinds of businesses. Louie explained all about the new themed restaurant that he was building. It would be completed in a few weeks. When the girls were sufficiently impressed, he knew the time was right to ask them if they would like to be a part of the Oceanside team. He explained that they would be rubbing shoulders with Miami's celebrities, politicians, and other VIPs. It would be great for their modeling career with so much exposure, waiting tables full of prestigious guests. When the girls asked if they could think about it for a day, Louie mentioned to them the amount of their pay, not including tips. They looked at each other, turned back to Louie with worshipful eyes opened wide, and asked when they could start helping him build his business.

As he was walking back to his place, it struck him once again how powerful and fortunate he was. He didn't have the physique of a body builder or the raving good looks of a movie star, yet he had just secured the services of two of God's best looking young angels in Miami. He barely resisted the urge to commemorate the occasion by making two snow angels in the sand. When he was a kid, the girls his age hadn't even given him a second glance, let alone even cared what he had to say. Now look at him! This struck him funny and he laughed. *Boy that felt good.* Then he thought about his happy family that was working hard on his home just to please him. The bad 'ole days of his childhood were far behind him. He couldn't muffle another laugh as he pictured the look on his dad's face as the police barged in to arrest him many years ago. He hadn't even thought about the security camera catching his face when the mask was pulled off by some hyperactive teenager. He laughed again, a little longer this time. He was living the lifestyle of the rich and famous. Then, he thought of his favorite cartoon when he was a boy. No matter how hard the wily coyote tried, he couldn't ever catch that blasted roadrunner. At the end, the coyote was always unwittingly holding a lit piece of dynamite before the explosion, or looking up at the anvil careening downwards to make a coyote-sized hole in the ground. *I'm the Roadrunner and the U.S. government is Wile E. Coyote!* This thought made him laugh the hardest. He felt tears falling from his eyes onto his cheeks. He was belly-laughing hard all the way back to his happy family. The thought ran quickly through his mind that he might be losing his marbles. If losing his marbles felt this good, he was willing to go along for the zany ride. He didn't even notice the mom and her six-year-old boy sunning themselves as he walked within inches of their spread-out beach towel. He had scuffed sand on them as he passed in his own delirium.

"Mommy, what's so funny" Jimmy asked.

"I don't know, Jimmy, but let's move down the beach a little farther," she said, pulling Jimmy close.

....

Of course, Heather and Molly had told all to Manuela, in a meeting that afternoon about the life-changing encounter with Louie. Manuela was the girls' agent and the owner of Manuela's Modeling. All her top young model hopefuls were there. It caused quite a stir and she promised that she would meet with this Louie and see if there would be other openings for her clients. Louie was thrilled to meet with Manuela when she called and yes, he did have more openings for both men and women, and yes, she could reschedule her early afternoon appointment and meet with him right now. He sent a limo for her. For lunch they had some of his personal chef's best cuisine in the outdoor dining area overlooking the gigantic pool, and the ocean waves a hundred feet farther.

Everyone was always taken with Louie. His big toothy smile, his jovial personality, and his laissez-faire attitude about spending money were charismatic. Of course they were even more taken with him if he sent some money their way. Manuela walked away more smitten by him than her two young clients had been. She had contracts for thirty models. Ten men were all to be buff, with one having scuba experience. Twenty ladies were to be tall and look great in a long mermaid-style dress, with five of them licensed for scuba. For the profit Manuela stood to make from their agreement, she was properly motivated to scour the area's gyms and beaches looking for the best looking twenty to thirty-year-olds she didn't already have as clients. There were many different nationalities represented in her choices. The top thirty were chosen for poise and how they looked in the Oceanside's prototype costumes. Louie was very pleased with Manuela's choices.

....

The Oceanside had been an immediate success. Opening night featured Miami's two hottest rising stars, singing and pulsating to their Latino dance beat in front of the big clam to a standing-room-only, frenzied crowd. Immediately after the concert, tables and chairs were brought in while the diners all took a tour of the grounds with Louie. Upon returning, the diners found their assigned tables, with their names engraved on the back of a small souvenir conch shell sitting on their respective plates.

The scene for the guests was dazzling: the aquarium was stocked full of exotic fish, the beautiful and flashy mermaids were weaving through the crowd taking food and drink orders, the Poseidon busboys, muscles rippling, were winking at the single ladies and causing quite a stir, and the steaming hot sea food was deliciously prepared by Miami's finest chef. The pristine surroundings of the ocean, sunset, and palm trees further added to the whole experience, making it a truly incredible evening to remember. Louie couldn't have dreamed of a more fantastic opening night. The Iranians soon started spoiling his fun, however.

Chapter Twelve

Sceva flew to Miami and met with Louie for lunch by his pool. After waving off a doting maid, Louie asked what this urgent meeting was all about. It seemed that Sceva's boss, whom Louie had never met, was demanding that he now include assassinations in his repertoire of espionage. He would be sent two Iranian-born, English-speaking professionals, Achmed and Jazira, already operating in the U.S., to be his assistant team leaders. Achmed would fit in at the Oceanside as the head waiter, and his partner, Jazira, would be the head waitress. Completing the team would be five Iranian hit men. Everyone would be there in three days. He was to hide them all in his mansion and provide for them until three assassinations were complete. The names of the targets would come soon. The Oceanside's private dining rooms with their separate entrances would be the perfect place to lure the unsuspecting victims. Reservations would then be deleted from the computers and the operations would be squeaky clean. Sceva and the higher-ups already had it all planned out.

Boy was this going to cramp his style! He would have to let all his servants go so no one would get suspicious and report them. He was going to have to bring his assistant team leaders into the Oceanside workforce because they would be instrumental in the operations. He complained to Sceva that he'd never signed up to be so directly involved in killing anyone. He felt queasy at the sight of his own paper cuts. He hated the thought of having to live with seven Iranian killers as his house-mates. Five didn't even speak English and he'd never tried to learn Arabic. *How do you even say, "Please pass the orange juice," in Arabic?*

He had told Sceva that he was going to have to pass on this one. Sceva told him that this one couldn't be passed. The two choices given to Sceva to inform Louie were: a pay increase to ten million a year and a five million dollar bonus when the three jobs were completed, or his head and body a mile under the surface of the Atlantic Ocean, each in separate places.

Louie had chosen the former without needing to think much about it. As Sceva headed out the door, back to his home country, Louie asked his chef to make him a drink, preferably something strong.

....

The first hit had been performed with precision. A Miami arms dealer had cheated a prominent government official in Iran out of seven hundred thousand dollars in weapons. When invited by a personal phone call from Louie to a private room during the grand opening month of the Oceanside, the man came with ten of his associates and guests. He was given the royal treatment, including a lethal dose of cocaine (which he was known to abuse from time to time) in his lobster bisque. When he started giggling and stumbling around, his guests knew he'd probably had a snort in the bathroom before the meal.

Then he started tugging at his clothes muttering gibberish and grabbing at people. As his heart exploded, he performed a perfect gut-buster landing with a thud a few moments later on the tile floor. A dark-skinned waiter rushed in and said he could take the heavy, limp man to the nearest hospital before the ambulance could get out to the Oceanside. All agreed, and he was taken to the hospital where he was pronounced dead.

A few days later, news reports stated that the man had succumbed to a lethal amount of cocaine in his system. This would be no surprise to his associates. Louie knew the man's partners and "friends" wouldn't want police snooping into his personal life, which might implicate them. He also knew the police would be happy. He hoped the police figured he got what was coming to him. *As they say, "the enemy of my enemy is my friend."*

After the success of the first plan, Louie was thinking that maybe he had misjudged the situation with his new accomplices. Achmed and Jazira were very astute professionals and, after all, he was just supposed to be leading and hiding everyone for a few months while the three projects were completed. Maybe he could overlook the toll his many houseguests were taking on his mansion and the claustrophobia of being tied to them. He could hang in there for a fat raise and bonus, couldn't he? Having to go to the grocery store every couple of days and pick up enough food for the ungrateful cohorts was getting to be quite the chore, though.

The second victim-to-be was a turncoat spy from Iran. He had come over to do the bidding of his government and report on the whereabouts and contents of two U.S. nuclear research facilities. He had gotten a taste of freedom, however, and was living the good life in Miami with the large amount of money he'd been given to buy supplies or to make bribes for information. He was set up by Achmed to join Louie's team, stay in the U.S. where he could enjoy his freedom and the discos he frequented, and all would be forgiven by the Iranian government. The deal would be done in a private room at the Oceanside over a feast of blackened Mahi Mahi and grilled jumbo shrimp.

The only two in the room were he and the beautiful Jazira, as Louie watched the scene unfold on the restaurant's security monitor. He could tell that the Iranian spy was more interested in Jazira and her mermaid outfit than the gourmet meal he was about to eat. She was seated to his left and was much too close to him. She was obviously way out of his league as he compulsively focused on her plunging neckline and the bountiful treasures found there. As they talked, he became more and more under her spell as she frequently touched his left shoulder, arm, and thigh.

Jazira told him Achmed had been delayed and would be arriving after dinner with the arrangements for his new living quarters at a beautiful mansion. There was a moment of silence, and then Jazira, pretending to be unable to control herself with the new recruit, leaned in slowly to kiss him. Her right hand moved up his left thigh, and then softly caressed his right cheek. She let her hot breath be felt as she pulled his face toward her, pressing her lips into his. His eyes closed for the last time as she let him feel the closest thing to heaven he would ever know. Her left hand, tightly clenched around the handle of a fisherman's knife, found its mark the first time. The blood drained from his chest as she breathed heavily with excitement, her eyes close to his, recording the shock and terror in them. She savored the moment.

Of course, since no one really knew the poor chap, no one knew to look for him off shore beyond the breakers. If they could even find any pieces of him after the sharks had their fill.

....

After this second victory, Louie should have been celebrating. *Only one more to go.* But, he couldn't shake this new nagging feeling that things were about to take a turn for the worse. It started with a recurring nightmare. In the dream, stock he owned in an Iranian company was shooting like a glowing star to the highest it had ever been. It was visible in the late-night sky, blocking out the other stars with its blinding glow as it climbed higher and higher. He was giddy with delight. He had all his associates, friends, his mother, and even his father - dressed in his correctional orange jump-suit - over to celebrate with him. A band was playing some heart-pounding high-pitched Arabic tune he had never heard before. On and on, the stock shot up, straight through the clouds, up to the sun. Even the sun's brightness was no match for Louie's star-studded stock. It soon became the sun! The party was now in frenzy mode with everyone shouting..."GO...GO... HIGHER...HIGHER... FASTER...FASTER...GO...   GO...HIGHER...HIGHER... FASTER...FASTER..." in unison, over and over for a very long time.

The only one who hadn't been drinking and yelling in excitement and admiration for Louie during the orgy of emotion was his mother. She was sitting at a table by herself, looking at a pic-ture of Louie when he was a boy. The picture was one she had taken of him after his first com-munion. He looked so proud, all dressed up and smiling with his wide, toothy grin. Louie looked a little harder at her soft face. Feeling the sudden sharp pain of a lifetime of regrets, he noticed that there were tears on her cheeks.

His attention was jerked back to the sun, however, when the band stopped playing and he heard the sounds of bewilderment coming from his cheerleaders. When the stock had become the sun, it fluctuated sideways there in a predictable pattern for a long while, like a heart monitor showing the peaceful blip of a well-functioning beat. The guests were relieved as they poured more drinks and the band started playing again, this time something appropriately soothing: "I Did It My Way." This was played three times and Louie mingled among the guests, getting congratulations and kudos. He even got to speak with his dad and tell him to watch out for those acne-faced teenagers next time he was robbing a bank. His dad thought that was one of the funniest things he'd ever heard anyone say and promised he would, slapping his son on the back.

At the end of the third time the song was played, he heard a couple of guests gasp. Then more gasping came from others. He wheeled around and saw with horror what was wrong. This stock, star, sun of his was falling out of the sky! What was worse, it was picking up speed as it went and was headed in their direction! There was nowhere to run or hide. It was just coming too fast. Some people headed into the house, some ducked under the table umbrellas. The only people who didn't move were Louie and his mother. She at the table, with her picture and tears, he standing in awe of the big sun about to obliterate him, everyone he knew, and all he possessed.

He woke up from this dream drenched in sweat every night for the last week, his normal jovial self, awash in a chest-tightening apprehension. It didn't help that his sleeping partners had gone from two of his voluptuous young maids to six rooms full of ugly, ill-tempered, bad-mannered, and messy Iranian death squad members. All except for Jazira, but Louie knew not to get near her. One tangle with her and he might not leave possessing what he so proudly came in with. He'd leave that to Achmed. The two of them seemed to be an off and on item. When the two were "on," he couldn't help but hear loud sounds of love coming from their master suite. After all became quiet again and everyone could get some sleep, Louie would smell cigarette smoke wafting under their door through his formerly non-smoking abode. Allergic to cigarette smoke, Louie would wake up the next morning with stuffed sinuses and a splitting headache to go along with his nightly nightmarish omen.

The house had become a wreck. For one thing, no one was taking out the trash. Since Louie had been the only one taking out the trash and his orders to Achmed to have the group help him went unheeded, Louie had given everyone an ultimatum. Either they help with the mounds of trash that a small army of Iranians could produce, or he would let it pile up. Evidently, cleanliness wasn't a strict part of their training, because the trash was quickly piling up. The halls were strewn with beer cans, empty potato chip bags, and fast food remnants.

He had also stopped trying to wash everyone's dishes after a few days, opting instead for paper plates, which were now becoming a part of the overall atmosphere of refuse. The palace pool was suffering as well. With no servants to stabilize the chemicals, the once crystal blue waters had turned a murky green. The bottom was nowhere to be found. The once lush, green, and well-cared-for lawn became overgrown. The various kinds of bushes and shrubs that adorned the property were now unruly as well. To top off the deterio-rating condition of his once immaculate place of solitude, the plumbing had backed up. Somebody had clogged up the basement toilet and ruined the use of the indoor plumbing. Louie wanted to call a plumber, but knew there was no way to hide what was going on in what had become his hell on earth. So, when the urge hit, everyone was now fertilizing the various overgrown woody foliage now turned latrines. It was only a matter of time until the strong smell emanating from just out-side the mansion's walls would crescendo into a disgusted neighbor's phone call to the city's nui-sance hot line.

Then, there was the question of who was in charge. Louie had been promised that he would have the authority in the group. But, the longer the time dragged on, it was quite apparent that Achmed and Jazira were running the show. Louie didn't know Arabic, and he had depended on Achmed to translate his commands to the troops. After only a few days into the project, he knew Achmed wasn't truthfully translating everything he was saying. When no one was doing anything that Louie asked around the house, the answer from Achmed was that the men considered it woman's work to take care of a residence. *What is Iran breeding over there, a bunch of barbarians?* Louie had raged about his broken magnificent crystal entryway chandelier, smashed during an indoor baseball game, the tattered nineteenth century sofa used in a mock stabbing lesson, and the gaping, jagged hole in the top window of the three-story living room, shattered when a silencer was being tested for noise level. The opening was letting in various kinds of birds to be sheltered and housed by landlord Louie. He never imagined seagull dung would accentuate his mansion's décor. None of his harsh English words had any effect on his housemates. There were only two who could even understand him. Achmed told him he needed to be more laid back and the men would appreciate him more. Besides, they only had one more job and they would be out of his life. Jazira always just smiled at him, soaking in the emotion of his anger. Feeling quite alone in a house full of strangers with Arabic music blasting in the background most of the day and night,

Louie wondered if he really was going to be able to make it until the next victim was eliminated.

Chapter Thirteen

The next target was Ames McCullough, the senior senator from Florida and a wise politician. He had sensed the public's growing frustration with Iran's harboring of terrorists who were intent on causing harm to the United States. He had recently proposed tightening UN sanctions against the country to wake up the dictatorship and maybe sway them to quit providing a safe haven. Iran's unofficial response was to make Senator McCullough the third target of Louie and his crew in the trio of unlucky victims. McCullough would be flying into Miami to speak to a group of Cuban Americans about the need for more diversity in the Florida legislature. The trip's goal was not only to try to gain some viable political candidates for his party, but to win votes for his re-election coming in twelve short months.

He was in high spirits as he had planned to be vacationing on the beaches of Miami for a few days after his speech. His secretary had been able to obtain reservations at the prestigious Oceanside on short notice! In fact, the restaurant had even contacted his office, knowing he was coming, and said they would be delighted to have him dine there, compliments of the management.

Louie had done a great job of making it appear that the dinner was a political pat-on-the-back that would be hard for any politician to turn down.

Things couldn't have gone worse with Louie's plan, however. He personally met his VIP at the main doors and escorted him into the restaurant and onto the stage. Grabbing a microphone, he introduced McCullough as the best senator Florida had ever had, spoke well of his astute political characteristics, and welcomed the audience to vote for his friend in the upcoming election. McCullough, quite pleasantly surprised by the flowery greeting, thanked his host's generous praise and made a mental note to frequent the place often when in Miami. He went on to thank the audience for their generous applause, and to speak shortly about his efforts to rid the world of terrorism. Before he relinquished the stage for the evening's entertainment, he spotted an opportunity to his right. Pointing to the aquarium, he couldn't help likening his opponent's ideas for national security to the naivety of the little red snapper swimming beside two vicious-looking sharks. Amid the audience's laughter and applause, he asked them for their vote in the coming election and left the stage. He didn't need a poll to know he'd just secured himself a room full of much-needed voters for his tight senate race.

Louie's plan was to throw off any suspicion from himself and the Oceanside by being so public and gracious. Also, there would be a comprehensive frame job by his team to implicate the other senate candidate as the perpetrator. A staged fight would take place when Achmed, standing by the front door, would rush out and tackle a masked Iranian sniper in the parking lot who had just put a bullet through McCullough's head. During the scuffle, a piece of scrap paper with the cell phone number of Congressman Simpson's campaign manager would fall to the ground in front of a restaurant full of witnesses. The waiting getaway car was an easily identifiable blue Camaro rented in the name of Simpson's biggest contributor. This was done over the phone with the contributor's stolen credit card number. The car would be ditched a couple of blocks away as the sniper switched vehicles and joined them later. Louie's simple but cunning plan had only taken him a few hours to implement.

Things started going south, though, when a waitress seated a couple that was next on the reservation list where McCullough and his press secretary, Pam, were to be seated. Jazira had been on her way with the senator and press secretary, when the senator asked to use the restroom. Pam said she should go as well and Jazira led them to the location in the front of the building beside the entry doors and the aquarium. She waited for them and when they rejoined her, she led them to the planned table. Not knowing what to do upon seeing the table already filled, and not wanting to cause a scene, she seated them two tables down. The mermaid's unknowing mishap made it impossible for the sniper to get a clear shot through the front glass windows at McCullough. Plan A was scrapped and a plan B had to be formulated in a hurry in the back of the kitchen between Louie, Achmed, and Jazira.

It was quickly decided that poisoning the senator's wine would be the best way to complete their job. Achmed explained about a new poison formulated by Iranian-government chemists that would actually cause a heart attack. He and Jazira always carried a few vials with them in case an imminent capture necessitated a quick suicide. It was well known that McCullough sported a pacemaker with a built-in defibrillator because of two previous heart attacks he had suffered in the last ten years. *Three times is a charm*, thought Louie. Louie congratulated himself on his good idea and the plan was put in motion. He wasn't going to let the botched operation keep him tied down to his house buddies for several more months in order to get another workable plan in place. They were going to do it right now. Was it possible that in just a few weeks he could be lounging by his pool, sipping a Mai Tai with no one else around except those that hung on his every word?

Jazira was already getting the vial from a small case in her purse.

Chapter Fourteen

The voluptuous, Jazira leaned over to the senator's ear, and with her hand on his shoulder whispered in her low, silky-smooth voice, asking if everything was to his liking. The senator, six months divorced, turned her way and took in the view. Looking into her beautiful brown, mesmerizing eyes six inches from his, made him light-headed. When his gaze melted down to her sequined top, he found his mind wouldn't formulate anything close to a syllable. She had waited on them at the restrooms and taken them to their seats, but he had not paid much attention to her in his euphoric state of emotion after doing so well at his impromptu speech. Now, the euphoria was back. Finally, after a few awkward seconds in which Jazira dangled the bait, McCullough hoarsely said, barely above a whisper of his own, "Yeah...I ...uh...like it very much." He dabbed his forehead and felt like a giddy teenager. Forget visiting the Oceanside on his trips to Miami, maybe he needed to get a condo close by.

His secretary, flabbergasted at what she was witnessing, turned the conversation to the more mundane topic of the need for more water. A quick glance at her glass by Jazira revealed that it was still three-fourths full.

"I tend to get real thirsty with dessert," she lied.

Jazira was off to fill the request, knowing the plan was working deliciously well, while McCullough watched her silhouette glide toward the kitchen.

"Be careful, Senator, I don't trust that woman," Pam warned.

"I thought I left my mother in Jacksonville," chided McCullough. "Besides, you need to get out more often; women are becoming freer to express themselves these days. If they want to freely express themselves to the senior senator from Florida, who can blame them?" *Man, I love the intangibles of this job. Serving the country is a tough gig, but somebody's got to do it.* He was grinning.

"Watch out who's freely expressing themselves to you, Ames, that's all I'm saying."

McCullough's eyes had veered right at the start of Pam's last sentence and Pam knew he hadn't heard a word she said. She shivered as Jazira slithered past her to her boss and she knew what the focus of McCullough's inattention had been.

Pam's frustration continued to grow. *Was it humanly possible to be back already with that freaking pitcher of water?*

McCullough, however, was very pleased with his hostess's quick service. Jazira never took her eyes off Ames as she filled Pam's glass. She set the pitcher down rather roughly by Ames and some water spilled out on his slacks.

"Oh, Senator McCullough, I'm so dreadfully sorry about that, let me help you." Jazira grabbed a napkin, got down on her knees beside Ames, bent over and began slowly rubbing the large water spot on his right thigh way too long.

Pam saw that McCullough was just sitting there under the mermaid's mysterious spell. Around the room, several voting diners nearby were beginning to take notice and whisper among themselves. She decided to take matters into her own hands.

I've got to get this guy out of here, fast, before this woman completely bamboozles him. She stood up and walked around to Jazira's back. "Thank you very much, miss, but it was just water, I'm sure it will dry," she said forcefully, while roughly tapping Jazira's bare shoulder.

For the first time in a while, the senator realized Pam was there. "Pam, she's just trying to help, don't make a scene."

Jazira stood up slowly, with McCullough's gaze again fixed on her every movement, and she turned, for the first time, to look Pam straight in the eye. A violent shudder of coldness swept through Pam's soul. She felt her hands shake. She could barely make out what the low voice of Jazira spoke to her in a breathless whisper: "You're right, Pam, everything will be just fine... soon."

Pam was just about to suggest to McCullough that they retire early for the evening and that she wasn't feeling well, but Jazira was already saying something to him. McCullough said he thought that, yes, it was a great idea to take a little tour of the grounds with Louie, as long as Jazira would be there for them when they got back to serve him dessert. Jazira assured him dessert had always been her specialty and that she wouldn't miss being there for the "grand finale" of his meal, catering to whatever appetites he had.

Then, she was gone. Louie was there in a few seconds, and Pam gratefully stepped out into the fresh evening air with the two men. Gradually, her head cleared from the bizarre actions of the cunning waitress and her willing boss. He had never acted so dopey before. After listening to Louie's voice rising and falling with great passion about this dolphin statue imported from Italy, and that mermaid fountain made by one of Miami's finest home-grown artists, and many other notable pieces of very expensive artistry, her nausea had all but vanished. With the beautiful sunset and the melodic peaceful sound of the waves rolling in, all was right in her world. The waitress had been overboard in her flirtations, sure, but who wouldn't be impressed by a single and powerful politician such as Ames? He wasn't her type, but then he did look kind of cute out here in this Miami sunset. *I've just been working too hard on this campaign, letting myself get worked up about things. An evil mermaid was after Senator McCullough?!* She almost laughed at her conspiracy theory. She'd leave those kinds of crazy thoughts up to the tabloids.

Their short, refreshing tour was over and they re-entered the Oceanside, and sat down at their table. It was now cleaned and set for dessert. Pam dreamed of having a hot, relaxing bath in her hotel room after she endured the rest of the mermaid's hormones, drank the rest of the tasty house wine, and enjoyed her free, delicious, twenty-dollar dessert.

Pam's happiness greatly increased when a waiter came and said their previous server's shift had ended. He said he was glad to be their new server and asked if they needed anything else to enhance their dining experience. The senator's mood was suddenly the opposite of Pam's, but he grunted that everything was okay. He wanted to know if their previous server had left any messages for him. The answer was "no."

Pam, not wanting to talk about the woman any more tonight, or ever again, for that matter, struck up a conversation about how they seemed to be leading a few points in the polls. Since Pam had finished her glass of house wine, she asked the senator if he'd mind if she drank his untouched glass. The senator had reluctantly given up drinking alcohol five days ago on his doctor's advice when he had changed his heart medication to something stronger.

"You may as well; it looks like there are a few pleasures I'm going to be missing for a while, anyway." Pam knew he wasn't really talking about the wine, but she decided to keep the conversation more positive and help her boss out of the 'mulligrubs,' as her mom used to say. She took a sip of his wine and noticed the taste was bitterer than hers.

"Oh, cheer up, Senator, this time next year you'll be starting a new six-year term and planning your campaign for pres...for pres..." Pam grimaced and grabbed her chest as it exploded in pain, spilling the red wine all over her skirt.

Louie looked on at the scene in horror from the kitchen, not yet realizing the full extent of the fatal mistake.

"Dear God! Are you okay, Pam?!" exclaimed McCullough. Seeing that she was definitely not, he yelled, "Someone call an ambulance!"

Chapter Fifteen

A team of heart specialists had worked on Pam all night before finally being able to get her stabilized. She was still in intensive care and wouldn't be able to communicate for at least another week because of all of her tubes and machines, but her life was no longer in immediate danger. What baffled the surgeons, though, was why anyone in such good health, with normal blood pressure and cholesterol, and no previous symptoms of heart trouble, could have such a massive heart attack. Because of their bewilderment, a battery of tests was conducted on Pam. In one of the blood tests, a strange substance was found and the results set off an immediate FBI investigation. The contents of her stomach were analyzed as well. They were found to contain the same foreign substance. Since McCullough told the investigators that the last thing she had ingested was the house wine, they also tested the stain on her skirt. The same poisonous substance was revealed. The implications were incredible. The news was kept secret from the public until the apparent crime could be fully investigated.

Pam was later told that if she had taken one more sip of the poison, the heart attack would've been fatal. If McCullough, which everyone surmised was the target of the poisoning attempt, had even had one drop of his intended beverage with his heart history, he would have died before his head hit the table.

It didn't take long before the FBI was on the trail of Louie Fisher. The chief investigator assigned to the case, Sam Bishop, had already perused the list of guests at the Oceanside on the evening of the debacle. It seemed that the owner had been a little too talkative, and smiled too much at their meeting, but was cooperative nonetheless. The guests were called in for questioning about the incident one by one at the main police station. Their backgrounds were meticulously researched. No one at the restaurant that evening seemed likely to perform such a risky, high profile, politically motivated murder. Lucky for Sam, the senator had everyone watching him and his secretary as they dined that evening. Those seated nearby the victim's table saw no one tamper with her food or drink. A few people reported that the waitress had spilled some water on the Senator and had tried to help him dry off, but the victim had told the waitress that it would be okay and she left. Most of the men volunteered that McCullough's waitress was very beautiful and seemed to be flirting with him. One of the nearby witnesses felt it necessary to tell Sam that he wished she would have spilled something on his pants and helped him get dry.

They all reported that the two had left with the manager or the owner for about fifteen minutes before returning for dessert. While they were gone, a waiter had taken McCullough's wine and both of their finished dinner plates. One witness, seated at the table behind Pam, with a full view of the couple, said that she thought it was odd that the waiter brought the Senator another glass of wine for dessert. She figured a public figure wouldn't want to be thought of as 'heavy on the alcohol.' The waitress did not return, but a waiter had taken her place. After he said something to the senator and his press secretary, he left. A few seconds later, people were yelling for the ambulance.

After the enlightening discussions with the twenty or so nearby witnesses, Sam began questioning the cooks, waiters and waitresses of the Oceanside. Sam felt like he was interviewing Mr. Universe and Miss America contestants. None of them had waited on the table in question. Most seemed very bright, with solid futures ahead of them. Their background checks uncovered nothing noteworthy. None, however, had anything good to say about their two managers, "Ace" and "Jazz." The employees had walked in on them many times either arguing vehemently with each other or torridly enmeshed in a search for one another's tonsils. They hadn't been very friendly with their subordinates, either. No one dared call in sick, come in late, or ask for an extra day off for fear of losing their jobs. With the pay they received, they all felt like it was worth enduring the dysfunctional autocratic style of management. Besides, the exposure to VIPs for many of their ultimate career goals was priceless.

Their attitude toward the owner was another reason they were attached to their jobs. It seemed that he had thrown many parties at his beachside estate for the employees, before the arrival of his new managers. Louie was looked up to by all. It also didn't hurt that the waiters and waitresses found each other to be very appealing company as well.

The investigation was narrowed down to Louie, Ace, and Jazz. Ace and Jazz had no records whatsoever. No birth certificate, no driver's license, no social security number, not even a credit card. Louie, however, had all these. Sam had a feeling that Louie was in on the attempted murder, but would need some time to study his background. He knew his suspects would try to flee the country if they thought he was getting ready to move on them, so he led them to believe the FBI had found the culprit in one of the interviews with the diners. Agents were to set up twenty-four-hour surveillance of Louie's estate. If they tried to flee, they were to immediately arrest them. For now, interviews with Louie, Ace and Jazz would wait until much more was learned.

In the meantime, CIA agents were brought in to try to coordinate intelligence with the FBI about the trio. Surveillance photos of Ace and Jazz were instrumental in identifying them. It was learned that Ace had arrived from Iran ten years ago under the name of Mohammad Al-Allundi on a student visa in order to study at New York University. He had never attended the school and never returned home. All that was known of his real name was Achmed. Six months later, Jazz had entered the U.S. in similar fashion. She was to study at a Midwestern university on a scholarship provided by a pilot program sponsored by the U.S. government. The program's goal was to help improve relations with Iran and for the U.S. to let a few of Iran's young people taste freedom at the same time. She majored in English, but dropped out a month before graduation, never to be heard from again.

Sam made good progress on Louie. His mother and dad were contacted. The dad didn't know much about Louie. He hadn't seen him in years. His mother prayed for him every night, but had no idea what had become of him. She had finally given up on him writing, calling, or contacting her in any way. If they knew where her son was, would they please tell her, so she could get in touch with him? They assured her that they would.

Sam got what he needed when he found that Louie had made a trip to Iran in college. After that, his standard of living seemed to rise significantly. His manager and a few old co-workers at the *Washington Daily* explained to Sam that Louie's parents were wealthy and would spoil him with family money. They didn't mind because he always shared it with them. Sam thought of old Mrs. Fisher in her rented studio apartment, barely eking out an existence on food stamps, and Mr. Fisher serving his tenth year in prison. "Yeah, his parents are certainly something," he had told them.

Chapter Sixteen

Louie was as nervous as a stray mongrel on the night of the Fourth of July. As of yet, the government had not suspected him of foul play in the botched attempt at Senator McCullough. In fact, the main investigator informed him that he thought he'd found the culprit. Still, being cooped up for the last two weeks with Achmed, Jazira, and the gang had taken its toll. They had decided that except for their normal shifts at the Oceanside, no one except Louie should go outside or leave the premises. Someone could easily be watching, keeping them under surveillance. Blinds were closed, curtains were drawn, and the phones were not to be used. This presented Louie with some managerial nightmares. Now, the motley crew couldn't even use the shrubbery to relieve themselves. So, he had to carry the five-gallon buckets of human waste to the ocean every night after dark. He was the only one who could get groceries. His once-beautiful landscaping was in a sad state of degeneration. And now he was going to need to completely remodel the interior of his home. None of his ungrateful freeloaders would pay one ounce of attention to anything he said. Louie wasn't surprised when he noticed his hair had started falling out.

The five imported hit men at Fisher manor were at each other's throats. Seclusion from the outside world was affecting their sanity. Two of the men had a vehement argument about one of their girlfriends back home. One tried to kill the other by choking him to death with one of the bedroom curtains. The others jumped the strangler and saved the weaker just as his face was turning blue. Another fight broke out when one of the men tried to take another's room because of its larger size. Knives slashed through the air, Arabic profanity spewed forth. After it was over, several deep wounds were stitched by the team's medic-killer. Achmed and Jazira seemed unfazed by any of this and kept to themselves in their psycho-neurotic, bipolar relationship. Louie was left to harness the chaos solo. He had now moved on from mixed drinks to straight whiskey, his shaky hands lifting the calming fluid to his eager lips while trying not to spill even one drop. He had eliminated ice from his drinks to get more per glass.

....

Sam Bishop had that feeling he got when he was closing in on his target. Some people felt it when they were about to close a very profitable sale, others got it when a large bet was riding on the hand and the first card dealt them was an ace. This hand was a once in a lifetime opportunity for Sam if all worked out well. His career would be capped with a major achievement and catapult him into lucrative writing or speaking opportunities beyond his impending retirement. If things didn't, he knew the remaining options offered to him after retirement would be few. The past couple of weeks had netted his surveillance team many crucial nuggets of information. With the newest, most sensitive listening technology available, the FBI recorded conversations between Louie, Achmed, and Jazira that not only linked them together in the poisoning attempt, but in two other secret murders. Louie had bragged that under his reporter's guise he had sources that would keep him abreast of any information he needed pertaining to politics, schedules, and other sensitive data, much of which was classified. The Arabic translator on the team, flown in from a U.S. naval station in Yemen, deciphered enough to know that there were five Iranian hit men holed up in the house as well. They had spoken a little bit about their role in the three recent crimes, but were concerned with getting out of the house and back to Iran. There were constant arguments and fights taking place. Now that he had the evidence he needed, Sam knew he must move in immediately or risk losing many of the perpetrators.

Louie hadn't had a good morning. He was out of vodka, more of his hair was covering the shower drain, and now he had learned the news that the FBI would be raiding his home tonight to make him pay for his sins.

A pretty young woman in black spandex, talking on a cell phone, pushed her stroller slowly down the street in front of the mansion for the third time and made one of the Iranians uneasy. The others poked fun at him, saying that he was just nervous and excited about the fashion boldness of American women. Irritated, he got out his well-worn, government-issue radio frequency interceptor. The woman's call was short but packed with dire information for the hold-outs. The woman was to end her surveillance assignment, tell all the others to do the same, and pull back to their base to watch for a possible escape attempt. At 6:00 p.m. there was to be a massive extrication operation to get the five Iranians. Then, they would raid the restaurant next, since Louie, Achmed, and Jazira were usually at the Oceanside by 5:00 p.m. every evening.

....

Louie, Achmed, and Jazira quickly made plans for everyone to abandon the house, taking everything necessary to sustain an all-out war. All that morning and afternoon, they organized their weapons and went over everyone's duties in what would be the fight of their lives. The Iranian five found it necessary to play their favorite wild-rifted, fast-paced, mind-numbing Iranian tunes loudly and repetitively.

When it was time to make their exit, Louie, not caring much anymore about trying to preserve unity in the group, stole a bottle of liquor from someone else's room and partook until he was buzzed. He grabbed a couple of his bewildered cronies and danced with them to the crazy beat. "What's wrong, can't dance?" he shouted above the noise. "Didn't teach you that in Murder 101? To hell with ya', then." Louie picked up the short man and threw him onto the ravaged sofa. Then he grabbed the battery-powered radio and threw it through a front window, glass and stereo crashing down on the walkway in the front yard. The music was still blaring. "Let's go!" he yelled to everyone in a high-pitched voice.

Hearing the distant commotion, a neighbor tinkering with her flower bed, ran inside and called the police, wondering if the neighborhood was going rental.

....

They managed to get all five Iranians in the trunk of the limo, leaving space for Achmed, Jazira, and the weapons cache in the main part of the car. Louie was driving. Everyone's windows were down to show no one else was with them. Other than leaving earlier than usual, nothing seemed different to their watchers. A tail was sent to follow and make sure the three stayed at the Oceanside until they were to be apprehended. Once there, Louie pulled into the drive for the storage building connected to the kitchen of the restaurant and punched the automatic overhead door button. The team exited the car and got to work in seclusion once the door had rolled back down tightly behind them.

At 6:00 p.m. sharp, the remnants of Louie's mansion were raided. The participants had never seen anything like it. The stench was incredible. Evidently the plumbing wasn't working because they found three buckets of sewage in the kitchen, two tipped over with their contents all over the floor. There was old food covering most of the rest of the kitchen, with mold and ants reaping the bounty. The furnishings were destroyed. They couldn't even see the floors because of the abundance of trash. After it was apparent that there would not be a fight or anyone to arrest, one SWAT team member jokingly remarked the scene was even worse than his college dorm days. Everyone loaded up and headed for the Oceanside.

Highly agitated that his prey had given him the slip, Sam was calmed somewhat by the report that Louie, Achmed, and Jazira were still at the restaurant. At least he could still get the ringleaders of the group. He couldn't afford any more surprises. There was tremendous pressure being put on him by the FBI, CIA, and even the White House to destroy or capture the terrorist ring.

PART 3

Chapter Seventeen

After listening to Louie's introduction of himself and the events that were to take place this evening, Tom and Sheila hoped they would be in the majority of guests that would be sent home. If not, they knew they would be in for a dire ride that might very well end badly. The group in the middle of the restaurant was all thinking the same thing. Why had they picked this evening to try out the famous dining destination? Husbands and wives held each other close. Kids clung to their parents. Harvey and Bortz felt like strangling Burton for suggesting the Oceanside, but they knew it wasn't his fault. Bunny was holding onto Burton's arm in a death grip.

Louie was pacing back and forth on the stage like a cat between two milk bowls. He scanned the audience as he held his finger over his mouth for a few moments. Everyone was looking at him, hoping fervently that they would be picked. To Harvey, it was similar to the playground memories of his youth. He would usually be chosen first or second any time there was a game of football to be played. This time there was a lot more riding on being chosen.

Louie was taking his sweet time. He finally started pointing to this one and that one and telling them to go stand along the entrance wall of windows. The windows were now dark, the blinds having been closed. He also had a little fun insulting a few along the way as he pointed out the winners. "You, in that ugly hair piece..., you, who would look better with an ugly hair piece..., the fat woman in tight clothes - we might actually have to move around a little tonight..., the old man that looks dead already, if you can even hear me..., you, sir, in that ridiculous 1980s outfit - did you think that we were going to 'Wang Chung' tonight?" Sarcasm had always been a specialty with Louie. He looked straight at Harvey, "Get out of here, Popeye; we already ate all the spinach."

Yes! Thank God, thought Harvey as he walked over to the wall to join the others.

Louie picked all of his loyal workers except two. He kept Heather, one of his first hires for the Oceanside, and Mike, the strongest of the waiters. Both would come in handy if he needed some helpers with experienced knowledge of the layout of the Oceanside. *Mike could also help with his brute strength and Heather, well, she just looks great in her mermaid outfit.*

He kept going for fifteen minutes, weeding the crowd down to the number he wanted while he enjoyed some sadistic fun in the process. When Sheila was chosen, all of a sudden the sinister mermaid stopped Louie and discussed the choice with him in hushed tones for a few seconds. Louie changed his mind and called Sheila back to the small huddle by the stage. As she walked back, her previous short-lived elation turned to a complete loss of hope for Chance with every step. Stuck in this situation, her visualization of any kind of miracle for her son was shattered.

A few more people were picked and then it was over. The relieved group along the wall was told to exit the building and leave the premises. No one had to be told a second time, as everyone moved as quickly as they could before Louie was able to change his mind. Except one. Harvey couldn't leave his best friend in this situation. As he slowly walked back toward the small group, guns were immediately trained on his large torso.

"Trade me for that big, hairy guy over there," he said.

"I don't do trades, stay right where you are," retorted Louie testily.

"No you don't, Harvey, I'll be just fine," was Bortz's stubborn reply. "Tell Sadie not to worry, that I love her and I'll be home soon."

"Oh, isn't this sweet, we've got a real touching and emotional situation here." Louie wiped a nonexistent tear from the corner of his eye. "What should I do, let the fat, hairy guy go so he and his wife can make big, hairy babies?" He was now walking around and looking at his captive audience as though he was before a grand jury. "Or, should I keep them both since they both seem to want to stay?" He paused a moment as if to actually think about it. "Well, who am I to stand in the way of friendship, Chevrolets, apple pie, and all that stuff? You *both* may stay, and may God bless America from sea to shining sea!"

An audible sigh of sympathy for Harvey came from many there. Harvey knew he could have just sealed his own fate for his friend's sake, but he had made up his mind while he was standing in the line to leave, that he could never have lived with himself if something had happened to Bortz, while he took the easy way out.

The weapons were dropped and Harvey joined the rest of the captives.

"To celebrate this joyous occasion for the ones of you leaving us, and to unify and initiate our new team members, let us now say the pledge of allegiance with committed hearts and lives. Heather, go get us something to use as a flag."

"Uh, we... we... don't have a flag, sir," stammered the visibly shaken young mermaid, looking frantically around.

"I said, get us something to use *as* a flag!" yelled Louie, causing most people to jump out of their skins at the sudden change in his mood and decibel level.

She ran over to a table, got a white cloth napkin, put a fork under it, and lifted it up. Heather walked toward Louie like she'd just come out of a foxhole, surrendering to the enemy.

"Will this do, sir?"

"Can you believe this girl?" he queried. "Such a beauty *and* a head on her shoulders!" He held the makeshift flag high in his right hand. "Alright, priest, you're supposed to be good at these sorts of things, start us off. Everyone better be putting their hands over their heart, too - I always got in trouble for forgetting." He turned to Achmed. "Shoot anyone who doesn't have their hand over their heart." Louie proceeded to put his left hand on his right side. No one dared to tell him his mistake.

Tom had never had this strange of an assignment before, but began in a strong voice that seemed to comfort the others. "I pledge allegiance to the flag of the United States of America..." Everyone joined in after a few words, except the nervous Iranians who had no idea what was going on, but kept their guns trained on everyone. Some of the captives were crying as they said the pledge. Their future looked grim; foreigners had their guns trained on them, and they were saying the pledge of allegiance to a madman holding up a white restaurant napkin.

After the final stanza, Louie had more instructions. "Oh, I almost forgot, we need to take up a collection! We couldn't have a proper meeting without letting everyone have a chance to give a little something of themselves. Besides, what we do is hard work and we need a little bonus money for our trip." He looked at Mike and Heather. "You two pass the plates, so to speak, with some containers from the kitchen. Start with the ones lined along the wall and finish with our little flock here in the middle. Make sure everyone is generous. Get their jewelry, wallets, pocket books, everything." He looked at the crowd with his large grin: "Remember, it is more blessed to give than to receive."

Followed by their Iranian chaperone, the two retrieved a couple of large metal mixing bowls from the kitchen and stopped in front of each captive to receive their valuables. Louie watched the proceedings intently. He more than once ordered Mike or Heather to pat down hostages to make sure they had given all. Sheila didn't have the money Tom had given her. In all the panic, she had left the envelope in her purse lying on the sand out by their table near the ocean. *Maybe they won't find it,* she hoped.

Those hopes were soon to be dashed, however. Evidently, Louie had thought there would've been some articles of value left behind in everyone's haste to make it to their little gathering. So, he ordered Achmed to tell two of his crew to make a sweep of the grounds where everyone was located just minutes before. After a few minutes, the men came back with many purses, handbags, cell phones, and other items. Sheila's purse was searched, and there, in plain view of everyone, a smiling Iranian held up the treasure high above his head.

"Well, well, well, what do we have here?" asked Louie. "Someone doing a little 'dealing' at my well-respected establishment?" He was half-mocking, half-genuinely impressed. "Achmed, get me the police! Well, maybe that isn't such a good idea." Louie enjoyed a hearty laugh at his own wit. His brow became furrowed. "Seriously, now... who brought in such a stash of cash into my restaurant?" He went animated once more. "I know inflation has gone up quite a bit recently, and, of course, we have had to raise our prices accordingly. But, I don't think it was necessary to bring that much jack! Mike, you were on our meal pricing committee – don't you know there are starving kids in... in uh... oh yeah, in Africa? You should be ashamed of yourself with people having to bring in this kind of dough just to eat here. Bring the money to me."

Achmed motioned for the Iranian to bring the money to Louie.

Tom couldn't stand the thought of Sheila not getting the money to help her son. He jumped out of line and tried to appeal to Louie. "I gave the money to a woman to..." Louie abruptly interrupted him.

"What do we have here? A priest giving a woman a lot of cash? This doesn't look so good. Naughty, naughty," mocked Louie shaking his finger back and forth. Two guards came and forced Tom back to his place.

"So who does this money belong to?" asked Louie, looking around at everyone.

After a few moments, Sheila owned up to her new, but temporary, possession. "It's mine and I need it more than you do," she replied, stepping toward Louie.

"Whoa, a beautiful woman and a wad of cash from a priest. Sometimes I think I'm in the wrong profession. But, not really. Was this a little hush-up gift? Or, maybe a down payment on something yet to come? Oh, it doesn't matter, because you're wrong about needing it more than me. No one needs it more than me!" Louie was now rubbing the bills on his neck and face. When he was done, he stuffed the money into his pockets with a big smile. "Try to come and get it, sweetie pie!"

Sheila was going to do just that. She got about halfway there, however, and was smashed in the back of the head by the butt of Jazira's gun. She fell full-body onto a table in front of her and slid across into the chairs on the other side. The chairs toppled over, taking her with them. She got up slowly, facing Jazira and several others pointing their guns straight at her.

"Oh, you guys are no fun at all," said a perturbed Louie to Achmed and Jazira. "Can't we mix a little business with pleasure? Haven't you ever played Hide and Seek before?" He turned to Sheila. "Sorry they messed up our game, darlin' but I'll have to take a rain check. I guess recess is over."

....

Sam and his squad were located across the street in the lobby of the Miami Sea Club Resort.

The wall of windows facing the Oceanside was the perfect place to view what was happening. They had commandeered the place the day before under the extreme protests of the manager and owner. All guests were relocated for safety. Once it was established that the government would be footing the bill for its regular occupancy percentage, plus a nice bonus, the owner capitulated and the team moved in. As he listened to the situation inside the Oceanside with his technology experts, Sam was a mix of emotions. The Iranian hit men were holed up in the Oceanside, and he had an incredible opportunity to capture one of the leading spies of his day. Louie, though, had somehow gained the knowledge that the restaurant was going to be raided tonight. He had taken hostages and Sam knew the risks to them were very high. In a standoff with authorities in these situations, he knew from his training that it would take a miracle for all of them to live through the battle. This fight would inevitably involve making some very tough moral decisions. This was the kind of scene that he had waited for his whole career. He was ready to prove himself. He was born for this. He gathered his team together and tersely said, "Get ready, it's going to be a long night."

Chapter Eighteen

The lucky ones were ushered out the front door of the Oceanside after being frisked for what money and possessions they had brought with them. It had been a small price to pay for what could have been their lives. Sam watched with binoculars from his vantage point across the street and immediately sent several agents to direct everyone over to the hotel. There, they would be screened for any pertinent information that would give the FBI some advantage in capturing their targets. Chairs were set up for them in the lobby and everyone was called up, in turn, to give their account of what had happened. It was the same story over and over again from all forty-one people: they were enjoying their meal when all of a sudden they were told to get to the center of the restaurant. Most of the people thought it was a joke at first, but when some machine guns were fired to hurry them up, they knew it wasn't a prank. They had been terrified that they were going to die at the hands of a madman, but were quite relieved to be released even though they had been robbed. Several commented that they were not going to take life so much for granted.

Sam learned that there were still twenty-one scared hostages in the building. From the interviews with the Oceanside employees, he learned that Mike Phillips and Heather Thompson were still being held captive. Also, a lot of people said that several wealthy looking people and a priest were among the twenty-one remaining. Sam felt a little better knowing a priest was among the captives. He was going to need all the chances for a miracle he could get.

As if Sam needed any more stress, as he was figuring out the FBI's game plan, three local news media teams showed up one right after another. They were asking to interview the released hostages, trying to broadcast from dangerous positions and asking agents questions while they were trying to concentrate on their jobs. Sam had Bill, his media coordinator, tell them they could interview the witnesses when they were released. They were also given a position in which to broadcast from inside the hotel on the second floor inside the ballroom. It was directly above the lobby with the same wall-to-wall tinted windows. No one was to enter or leave from the main entrance, only the back one. The local news crews were nervous and excited to be there and they were especially pleased to get such an excellent vantage point. They knew they couldn't have paid for a better rate-boosting drama. They were clanking their equipment onto elevators, running massive cords up the stairwell, and talking excitedly as they were running around, setting up for what was going to be the story of the year.

A couple of trainees came slowly pushing a cart full of heavy media equipment through the front door before anyone could warn them of how easy a target they were for the machine guns across the street. Bill, expecting a burst of enemy gunfire, yelled, "Get inside and get down *now!*" The boys immediately flew down, thinking that maybe the enemy had now set up camp in the Miami Sea Club Resort and they were being added to the hostages. In their hasty reaction, the cart they had been pushing was shoved forward into the large mass of cords and feed lines snaking across the floor disappearing up the stair well. The top-heavy cart tipped over with a metallic crash, scattering pieces of shattered glass and equipment parts all over the large tiled lobby. Sam was livid. He stood up and bellowed to everyone within earshot, "We've got a national crisis going on across the street with twenty-one innocent lives hanging in the balance and I'm dealing with the damned Barnum and Bailey Circus all around me! Everyone, shut the hell up, quiet the hell down, or get the hell out!"

Everyone stood in shocked silence for several moments, including Sam's team. He had just established himself as the authoritative leader of the United States of America against the terrorist group from Iran and it was a sweet release. He barked to the metro-looking anchorman who had been waiting on the cart's cargo, "Grab a broom pretty-boy and clean up this mess." Then he turned to his team, still silent from the outburst. "Get back to work, we've got a job to do." Heads and arms jolted instantly back to their equipment.

When Bill thought Sam had cooled down a bit, he warned him, "It will only be a couple of hours before the national media will be crawling all over the place as well." He had barely spoken the warning to Sam, when someone said excitedly, "Look, two people are coming out of the restaurant! One has a gun!"

....

After the diners chosen by Louie had exited the restaurant, there was an extremely lonely feeling that came over the twenty-one hostages remaining. They were now the focus of the madman. He broke them up into two groups of eleven and ten to further isolate them and fulfill his plan. Tom, Sheila, Harvey, Heather, and seven others were told to move to the kitchen. Jazira took three of the Iranians with her to help guard their captives. Bortz, Mike, Burton, Bunny and six others were told to get under the back deck. Achmed took his other two team members and guarded them.

Louie grabbed some extension equipment he had brought with him and moved one of the restaurant's massive speakers into the front doorway. The speaker would allow Louie to communicate with his pursuers while also allowing the air to circulate. He had shut off the air-conditioning in case someone would try to put a sleeping gas through the ventilation system. The temperature was already climbing. He asked Jazira on their headset communication system to open the back door as well, to try to keep the heat down in the restaurant. She had already complained from the kitchen that they were going to fry if something wasn't done soon. Jazira scoffed at having to perform such a menial task, but left her post with her eleven captives, walked past the large shell and threw open the door, almost shattering the glass from it. She banged a chair against it to hold it open and stomped back to her assignment. Instantly, a draft of the evening ocean breeze blew through the place offering a welcoming drop of temperature. The kitchen windows were also opened delivering the soothing gift to the hot and suffering captives. Louie muttered something off headset and barely audible, about Jazira picking a fine occasion to have her time of the month. Jazira shot him a look at which the devil himself would have cringed. He battled a strong urge to detonate the death vest of explosives he was wearing in order to rid himself of her, but instead, grabbed his satellite phone and called Sceva. The team's rescue plans were finalized and Louie felt a bit better.

With Jazira gone for a few minutes and the loud distraction of the banging door taking place, the concentration of the three other captors in the kitchen was broken. They were still keeping an eye on their eleven captives, but they were talking quickly back and forth to each other. This gave Tom a chance to size up his fellow entrapped men and women. All of them had been herded between two shelves of produce and ordered to sit on the cement floor. Beside him was Sheila, glaring ahead, jaws clenched, like she could, at any moment, smack a captor in the face and not care when she died from the ensuing bullet. Beside her was an older couple that looked like tourists from Texas. They were wearing matching embroidered shirts and were sporting cowboy boots. The boots they were wearing were very nice, but well worn. Even though they looked like they were in their late sixties, they were in incredibly good shape from a life of farming, Tom deduced. *Probably wishing they had just vacationed at a nearby lake instead of ending up in this mess in Miami.* Next to them was a professional-looking woman looking very awkward sitting on the floor in her knee-length blue dress and matching high heels. Tom saw the ring on her finger and knew her husband must be incredibly worried about her. To her left, and directly across from Tom, was a kid who looked about fifteen. He was the only younger hostage left. He had a nose ring and several tattoos on his arms. His hair was spiked and colored blue to match his lipstick. He had probably come with his parents, thought Tom. Even though the kid was as nervous as everyone else, he was keeping an eye on the beautiful mermaid to his left. Heather's eyes were filling with tears that she was obviously trying to fight. She wasn't succeeding. It was apparent to Tom that she had been tricked into this whole Oceanside deception. Beside her was an athletically built, all-American-looking man. Tom had exchanged a few remarks with him as they were being funneled into the kitchen and had learned his name was Harvey. He was trying to soothe Heather. "It's going to be okay. This will all be over soon." Their guards heard Harvey and one gave him a stern warning in Arabic with a gun to his head. Meanwhile, Jazira came stomping back to the group in a foul mood. This cut short Tom's survey of the group, except to glance at two Japanese tourists beside Harvey and a Cuban-American between him and the Japanese. Everyone sat in silence for a few minutes until Tom could see, through the propped open kitchen doors, Louie pushing a frightened lady at gunpoint through the front door of the restaurant.

Chapter Nineteen

Burton had been knocked out cold and was now lying across the lap of Bortz, who was trying to revive him. There was a trail of blood oozing from his right temple. Achmed, acting upon some message received through his headset had, without warning, come up to the group under the large deck, grabbed Bunny and ripped her from Burton's grasp, pulling him from underneath the sandy prison. Burton had valiantly tried to wrestle Achmed, but he was no match for the large killer. For good measure, one of his cronies cracked the butt of his machine gun over his head. At least Burton didn't have to experience the drama about to unfold surrounding his beloved wife. Looking up through the weathered boards of the deck, Bortz could see the handoff from Achmed to Louie. Bunny had been flailing and hitting and Achmed had been half-carrying and half-dragging her. When she was given to Louie, he said something sternly to her that Bortz could not hear. She immediately began cooperating with him.

....

Illuminated in the police spot lights, Sam noticed the man coming out of the Oceanside looked as though he was on a tropical vacation: ready to play a round of golf or maybe just sit beside the pool while perusing the latest issue of his favorite financial magazine. He had on a Hawaiian print shirt flapping in the breeze and khaki shorts with matching boaters - no socks. He also had a few too many gold chains of various sizes around his neck. The woman's demeanor was entirely different. She looked haggard. Sam could tell from her ashen face and reddish-stained eyes that she was terrified for her life. She had good reason to be. There was a handgun to the back of her head as she walked in front of her captor in unison with him to the center of the street.

Sam had already set up a solid bullet-proof blockade in front of the glass windows of the lobby. Many of his sharp-shooting team was sta-tioned there. Others were stationed on various floors of the hotel as well as the roof. There were still others down each side of the street. The street itself and all the surrounding avenues had been blocked off hours before. Until now, there had been nothing moving on the otherwise bus-tling beach thoroughfare except for a few pages of the newspaper resting in the rocking hands of the ocean breeze.

While he had been waiting for Louie to make his demands known, he had afforded himself a quick remembrance from his youth. In this same area, twenty-five years ago, he had had his best vacation ever. His dad had announced to his mother and sister that he was going to take him on a "men only" vacation. He was twelve at the time and just being called a man was a thrill. He and his dad had spent a whole three-day weekend fishing from the dock, swimming, playing catch, throwing the Frisbee, and hanging loose together. They had eaten their lunches at the little sea-food stand on the dock. His dad had been very busy with his small meat shop and had decided to give Sam a treat and have some real father-son talks. Six months later, his father was killed in an attempted robbery of the family store. Sam would always remember that weekend with his dad. It had been the highlight of his life. The way in which his dad passed away had played a sig-nificant role in his decision to fight against the evil in the world that tore apart what was dear and sacred. Even though his reminiscences of the long ago weekend were his most precious thoughts, they were even more so now that his own son was nearing his twelfth birthday. He had told Jimmy that he would take him in a couple of weeks on a father-son camping trip down the beach to the state park for his birthday.

The sight of Louie nonchalantly playing with the life of someone's wife or mother made his blood turn to ice. *Easy now, keep a clear head, this might be a long ride.* Sam steadied himself. *Let's hear this idiot's request, and then look for an opportunity to rid the earth of him.* Even now, the sharp shooters had their precision weapons trained on Louie's head in case the situation turned into an all-out-battle. They were waiting on Sam's order to end Louie's life with a single shot. Sam and Louie knew, however, that the hostages would be immediately killed if this took place.

....

Louie took a moment to savor his bargaining position. He had idealized the "bad guys" of the many westerns he had watched when growing up. They would hijack passengers on a wagon trail, or ride into town and rob a bank, or break someone out of jail. They always seemed to blow a lot of things to smithereens in their escape attempts. Far too many ended with his heroes getting caught, so he would just keep watching the sections in the beginning through the middle of his videos, and then shut them off toward the end.

He held all the power. The posse was after him, but he couldn't be touched. As he took in his surroundings, he realized how quiet everything had become. The only sound was the intermittent gusts of the ocean breeze. It was a similar sound he heard when he put a large seashell to his ear.

What a beautiful evening. Too bad all the lights were on. He pulled his designer sunglasses out of his shirt pocket and slid them on over his ears. He knew the national media had arrived and would be broadcasting the whole escapade, world-wide, in real time. Through the lights, he could even see the silhouettes of their cameras on the second floor, trained on his every move. He instinctively smoothed his wind-blown hair with his free hand and flashed his winsome smile to the news organizations. They were going to be part of his leverage campaign to win his freedom. He couldn't have asked for more complete coverage of his plight.

Louie cleared his throat as if to begin the first note of an opera and turned on his microphone connected to the loud speaker. "I'm ready to deal with the man in charge. Come out unarmed, so we can do business."

"Do you want me to go out and talk to him?" asked Bill.

"No, I'll do it," replied Sam, already walking to the door. As he stepped out the entrance to the hotel, he held his hands high. He felt as though he was striding toward a world-wide stage. Not only were many people counting on him for their very lives, this was the most important assignment of his career. There were the blinding stage lights, the millions watching, and the high drama of life and death hanging in the balance. He knew there were machine guns trained on his every step. *Oh God, help this thing to turn out alright.*

As he got closer, he noticed the hostage more clearly. She was wearing a very expensive designer dress, high-heeled shoes, and had the demeanor of a wealthy woman. However, she was scared out of her mind and her eyes pled with Sam to help her.

Louie was overjoyed at how Act One was unfolding. *This is just like high noon at the OK Corral*, he thought excitedly. He resisted the urge to quickly shoot Sam and the woman and die with glory in the spotlight while the world watched on their television screens. *Get a hold of yourself. When I escape, I've got a lot of livin' it up to do.*

"You've backed yourself into a corner," said Sam as he neared Louie.

"Shut up, I'll be the one talking here. Grab your note pad. I'm going to give you instructions on how you are going to save everyone's lives and help my team and me escape. If everything is not followed perfectly, everyone dies, including this rich little beauty." To emphasize his point, he grabbed Bunny's hair with his free hand and pulled back her head in a violent jerk. His other hand still pressed the hand gun to her temple. Bunny let out a quick scream. Louie knew that he had been smart to give a face to all the other hostages by bringing someone out to demonstrate the seriousness of their plight.

"Now, don't be hasty, I'm sure we can work out something," replied Sam. He pulled a note pad from his shirt pocket.

"Smart man. I need a Huey Helicopter, fuel tank topped off and fully armed, delivered here before 9:00 a.m. day after tomorrow. Set it down on the beach side of the restaurant. The only one on board should be the pilot. He is to get out and stay. We will take a hostage with us to ensure no one will follow us or harm us. It will be their lives for our lives. We will release the hostage at our convenience and in our timing. The hostage will not be harmed and will only return safely if my instructions are followed precisely. Any questions?" Louie had the smile of a physics professor after delivering a smooth discourse on the theory of relativity.

"What if I can't get you the helicopter by 9:00 a.m.?" Sam asked, testing him.

"Then someone like this little lady will die," Louie answered while jerking on Bunny's hair a couple more times. "In fact, I think it will be *this* one." His winsome smile had turned into a deranged, curled smirk. Bunny had tears running down her cheeks and her eyes asked Sam for more than he could give.

To calm them both down a bit, Sam said that he would get right on the request.

"Great, that's all for now." He and Bunny backed away with her still in front of him until they both were back inside the Oceanside.

Chapter Twenty

An idea had hit Sam in the middle of the night that he dared not dream could work. Could an international terrorist incident be averted because of the love of a mother? He certainly hoped it could at least help.

"Mrs. Fisher?" Sam queried as he heard a sleepy voice answer his call.

"Yes, who the blazes is calling this time of night?"

"Mrs. Fisher, this is Sam Bishop from the FBI down in Miami."

"Well this better be something worthy of waking me at this hour – I'm sure my good-for-nothing husband didn't break out of jail."

"Yes Ma'am, this is a very important call. Did you watch any television this evening?"

"No, there's never anything I want to see from those Hollywood hippies."

"Well, your son's in a lot of trouble, Mrs. Fisher. I think you are the only one who can help him and all of us through this."

"What's Louie into now?"

Sam told her the gravity of situation. She asked for some time to get her thoughts together. About an hour later she called back and was told the FBI was to pick her up in a helicopter and deposit her right on the center stage for what would hope-fully be a peaceful, final act to the drama. Sam knew it was a long shot, but every once in a while, long shots worked. The alternative could be an unimaginable human travesty.

Sam had rigged up his own communica-tion device placed on the roof of the hotel. He had some help from one of the tech guys from a local news crew in assembling a huge bullhorn that projected his voice from a hand-held C.B. He blasted a message to Louie and told him that his mother had asked to see him one last time before he left the country for good. Using a little reverse psychology, Sam said he wasn't inclined to accept such a request, but since Louie was holding quite a few hostages, he would let his mother visit if Louie would release someone.

Jazira and Achmed had vehemently refused to entertain the idea of Louie's mother coming and the unintended consequences that might bring. Louie, haunted by his dreams and the thought of never again seeing the only one who had ever loved him, told them that he was still in charge of this mission. He said that he'd sabotage the whole mission if they couldn't be a little flexible with him after all the hell he'd been through, accommodating them over the past several weeks. Louie sent for the professional lady in the kitchen and he communicated the horse trade via his amplified speaker.

Sam was relieved that he had procured the release of a hostage and was hoping against hope that bringing in Louie's mother might be a miraculous solution to the end of the standoff.

The lady's husband, in a cordoned off area in the hotel for the hostages' relatives, was ecstatic. He was just telling someone how they had recently celebrated their twentieth anniversary at the Oceanside a couple of weeks ago. His wife had been so impressed at her husband's restaurant choice, she had returned to do some research for the Culinary Institute of Miami's "The Future Tastes of Miami" monthly feature article. She was a freelance food writer for several different food and restaurant publications. The man learned about his wife's release just as he finished his story to another hostage's relative. They both had broken down at the end with the knowledge that they might never see their loved ones again. His tears of loss had turned to unbelievable joy. Others around him were congratulating him, and at the same time wistfully wishing it had been their loved one. But, if she had been released, maybe their wives, husbands, or parents would be released soon. Their general mood was greatly improved and a ray of hope crept into their hearts.

That evening, Louie's pulse quickened as he heard the helicopter approaching. The roar got louder and louder in sync with his heartbeat as he knew his mother would be stepping off the craft any minute. As it touched down in the middle of the blocked off street and she jumped down onto the pavement, his throat tightened, making his breath labored. He hadn't seen his mother in almost twenty years. Louie whispered a wide-eyed "Momma." A flood of memories struck him and his eyes stung in the wind. He wiped them several times as he looked through the chopper window at the woman who gave him birth, nursed him, and had been the kindest yet strongest presence in his life. In fact, no one had ever loved Louie except for Momma. Not Dad, not Louie's paid-for friends, not his employees, and certainly not his recent housemates. *Dear, sweet Momma.* She wasn't a thing of beauty to anyone except Louie. She was a well-worn large-boned woman with strong features, but to Louie, she was the most beautiful woman that God had created. There had been only one woman's true love in his life.

As Isabelle Fisher stepped out of the chopper, a swirl of wind almost ripped her wide-brimmed hat from her head and it was only saved by her quick reaction, clutching it back onto her crown with her forearm. In a short moment she was across the street and into the arms of Louie. They had a long embrace. The warmth that touched Louie's soul had not been felt in many years. He resisted the urge to ask for cookies and milk.

"Mom, I'm sorry, I've not been a good boy - I'm in a hell of a fix."

"Damn straight you are." She put her arm around Louie as they entered the Oceanside. Her voice bellowed, "How did my sweet little Louie that I sent off to school every morning with a kiss end up in a mess like this? First, your father and now you. I broke my back to make sure you wouldn't turn out like him. I worked all day waiting tables while your father sat in jail, and most nights I read to you until you fell asleep. I had such high hopes for you - saving every hard-earned penny for you to go to that college." She was looking past him and around the restaurant.

"I'm so sorry, Momma."

"Is this your restaurant?"

"Yes, Ma'am."

"I bet this place looked real nice at one time, son."

She caught a glimpse of the group of hostages with Sheila and Tom through the open kitchen door.

"Dear God, Louie! What do you plan on doing with these people?!"

"Momma, don't be mad, I'm in a real fix. It's either me or them. They're my get-out-of-jail-free card. I won't disappoint you. You won't have to come visit me behind bars, like you did Dad. I'll never let that happen - never."

"I'd still much rather visit you behind bars than behind a headstone."

"The plan isn't to hurt anybody, but to live out the rest of my days in peace. This is my last gig, Mom. I think Dad would have been proud."

"The only way it can work out, Louie, is if you walk straight out with me, like a man, and surrender."

"I went too far this time. They don't let people like me surrender. But I promise you this, I'll make you proud."

He embraced her one more time, smelling that sweet, familiar fragrance he remembered as a boy.

"I know there's good in you, son. I can feel it."

"You...you have to leave now, Momma," Louie stammered, looking down. "But, I won't let you down, I promise." His eyes were giving him trouble again, tears threatening to brim over onto his cheeks.

She grabbed his hand, while her piercing eyes searched his. "Deep down, I know you're a good boy."

He pushed her gently, but firmly, out the door and watched her get back in the helicopter, knowing that this was the last time he would ever see her again. He watched her go higher and higher until he couldn't make out her form any-more - still waving long afterwards. "I'll make you proud, Momma," Louie whispered into the sky.

Chapter Twenty-One

"Alright, let's get this dinner show on the road!" Louie proclaimed, once back inside his shelled-out restaurant. "We've got a long ways to go and a short time to get there." Louie loved to say this line ever since as a kid he'd seen *Smokey and the Bandit* seven times during the first two weeks of the movie's debut. The theme song was as ingrained in his mind as his insatiable need for importance. *Bandit would pee his pants if he had this many smokeys after him!*

"Achmed, inform the group out back that they'll sleep under the deck for another night. You take three of your crew and guard them. Jazira, you take two of your people and guard the hostages in the kitchen again tonight. Make sure everyone remains alert, and sleep in shifts. If anyone tries to escape, kill them immediately - we have no room now for mistakes."

This was it. In the morning the plan would either work or it wouldn't. If it did, Louie would be living a princely life with the people who raised him from being a pauper. If it didn't, well, it would be one hell of a fireworks show. Either way, it was going to be quite the promising drama, Louie concluded. The only thing that kept tugging at him like an after-pepperoni heartburn was his mother. He couldn't forget the look she had had on her face as the helicopter had whisked her away. She had seemed so disappointed, so sad. *Why couldn't she be proud of me just this once?*

Louie shoved these lingering thoughts out of his mind. There was a lot of work to do by morning. He also needed to get his beauty sleep so he could be in his best form for the cameras tomorrow.

The drama between Louie and his mother had held the attention of the captors. Tom, Sheila, and the other hostages in the kitchen were able to whisper to each other enough to hatch a simple escape plan. This was far better than, for all they knew, certain death. Ward, the Texan tourist, had said that he'd be hog-tied before a few foreign farts would be allowed to harm his wife or himself, or for that matter, anyone else in their company. He'd spent eight years in the Marines and believed they had a chance to overrun the Iranians guarding them. With a little luck and a little help from the man upstairs (a nod toward Tom's direction), they'd walk out battered but still alive. Ward sounded confident. Harvey, Tom, and Sheila said they were in and then everyone else signed on to a plan that Ward had been thinking about. Anything was better than waiting around riddled with anxiety, helplessly wondering if every moment was their last.

After dark, Jazira went to join Louie, and Achmed, who were talking by the back porch and keeping an eye on the hostages there. She sent the rest of the guards except one into the kitchen to beef up security there. During this guard exchange, Ward motioned with his eyes for the kid seated in their group to go into action.

"I've got to pee so bad, I'm going to explode!" he proclaimed while holding his groin.

A few retorts went back and forth between captors. A disgusted guard was relegated to the task of taking the kid to the bathroom. As the two left, the number of their guards went down to three. It was the Texan couple's turn in the spotlight.

"We have not been to thirty-five states of this great country of ours, we've been to thirty-six!" exclaimed Ward to his frustrated-looking wife.

"You're thinking of Alaska, and I've already told you that I've never been there. You went by yourself on that ridiculous fishing trip with a couple of your buddies the first year we were married, under my direct protest!"

"No, I'm not talking about our first year of marriage." Ward ratcheted up the argument. "Don't you remember when we went across the border for a few miles to get something to eat when we were doing our Canada driving tour? Man, do you have a short memory."

The Iranians were getting agitated as people kept talking. "Short memory?... short memory!

Who's got the short memory? Wasn't it you who forgot my birthday last month?!"

A guard was now right beside Ward on one knee, trying to get his attention to shut him up.

Ward motioned toward Harvey as if to draw him into their spat. "You'd of thought that I'd have served her divorce papers! I forgot one little day of the year and now I'll never hear the end of it. I even brought her to the Oceanside to make it up to her and now look at what it's got me!" As Ward said this, he gestured hard with both hands as if to show his listeners the entirety of the Oceanside. As he accurately predicted, the back of his large right hand smashed into the guard's face, sending him reeling onto his back, firing his weapon into the air. Harvey immediately lunged forward beside the man and pushed him onto his side away from the group, firing the gun toward another guard. A bullet struck one of his legs as well as the restaurant's flour storage. The Japanese couple and the Cuban-American ran to their posts, very glad to get out of there. The quick action had thrown the other two terrorists off guard and one dove behind a counter to regroup. The third had been so startled with the intense gunfire smacking items all around him, that he flung aside his gun and ran for cover into the meat locker off to the side. Harvey wrestled with his foe, trying to free the gun while it was still firing willy-nilly all over the kitchen. Harvey then felt the bullet-proof vest on the guy and decided on a different tactic. Still overpowering him, he picked the guy up, and with both arms around him fired the gun toward the place where the guard dived behind a nearby counter.

Pots, pans, and all manner of produce from the three stationed in the back were now also raining down behind the counter. The plan was working, but Harvey couldn't hear Heather's cry warning them that the female captor was running back toward the kitchen.

Sheila heard, however and slipped to one side of the French doors. As soon as the doors exploded inward, she threw a front kick, breaking the nearest door off the hinges, knocking Jazira up against the opposite wall, her gun ricocheting out of her hands and out of reach. She slumped to the floor, dazed and bewildered. Wasting no time in taking advantage of her surprise attack, Sheila rushed forward to deliver some more pain. She pulled Jazira off the floor by her hair and was about to break her nose by slamming her head into her knee, but Jazira instinctively grabbed Sheila's foot and jerked it out from under her, landing her on her back, knocking the wind out of her.

Jazira lunged for Sheila, landing on top of her, pinning her to the ground. "I'm so glad you wanted to play, because I'm queen of this game!" Jazira hoarsely whispered in Sheila's ear. Sheila spat into Jazira's eyes and the two struggled, rolling a few times until Jazira was able to get Sheila into a leg lock. "You'll regret that... now, feel the pain!" Jazira couldn't care less about all the gun fire and confusion. She was raging with anger and all that mattered was making sure Sheila died after suffering as much as possible.

Louie, Achmed, and Jazira had been keeping an eye on their hostages under the deck while discussing plans for the following morning when they had heard the gunfire from the kitchen. Louie had immediately barked to Jazira to see what was happening. After a minute of suspense, he told Achmed to keep watch on this "outside" group with the other guard and make sure no one moved. Then, he raced to the kitchen to see what was going on.

As he got there, he stopped at the opening to the kitchen, and realized one of the doors was missing. It was a minute or two before he could make out what in the world was happening. There was a cloud of flour in the air covering everything. Gunfire seemed to come from everywhere and people were yelling in two languages. He could make out Jazira and one of the women captives in a life and death struggle on the floor. They were covered in flour as well, hair flying, clothes ripped. Louie barely resisted the urge to yell, "Cat Fight!" He could have immediately run into the situation and tried to shut it down, but he had a couple of reasons to let it play out. The most important reason was personal preservation in a dangerous situation. The second was that he had a front row seat, watching two beautiful women in an amazing struggle that was far better than any pay-per-view action he'd ever seen.

Jazira was now choking Sheila to death, still on top of her, knees pinning her arms to the ground. With Sheila's life fading, she knew Chance didn't have any hope without her. She thought of him for a second lying in the hospital all alone, with no one to care for him as he died. *I'll never let this witch take me from him!* She mustered all her adrenaline and strength, raised her legs high into the air behind Jazira, rushed them forward, crossing them in front of Jazira's neck and head. Then, she flung her body out straight, snapping Jazira's head and body back while ripping her hands from her neck, claws leaving a bloody wake. Jazira's head hit the cement floor with a loud smack! Sheila stood up, quickly regrouped and grabbed a pan on a nearby counter. She raised it high above her like an ax and brought it down with all her strength toward the intended target of Jazira's face. Jazira barely rolled out of the way as the steel pan hit the floor and sent shock waves through Sheila's arms.

Tom, upon seeing Jazira's gun slide to a stop on the floor, had grabbed it and headed toward the meat locker to take care of some business. He opened the large steel door and was met with the cold air but had no sight of his adversary. He noticed some floury footprints leading behind some hanging meat toward the back.

"Get out here where I can see you!" Tom called.

Silence.

Pointing the gun toward the largest side of beef where the prints ended, he let out three quick bursts from the gun into the hanging carcass.

"No shoot! No shoot! In Bible say turn other cheek!" the man said tersely, holding his hands up and emerging from behind the meat.

Tom walked stealthily towards him with the gun trained on his chest, his gaze steady. "Haven't you ever heard in Bible that if you spare the rod, you'll spoil the child? Well, I got a little bit o' rod for you, my child!" As Tom said this, while approaching the man, he smashed the side of his gun into the man's temple, knocking him out cold and into shelving of all sorts of food supplies. The shelves and supplies came down on him with a crash. Tom, satisfied that he was out of commission, went to lock him in and join the others in the rest of the fray.

As the flour died down a little more, Louie could see what was happening more clearly. He decided that he'd better step in and help Jazira. Sheila had her back to him and was bringing the large pan back above her head to try to smash Jazira again. Louie's thoughts had been on a commercial he remembered from when he was young. Seeing Sheila wielding the pan reminded him of the jingle, "*She can bring home the bacon and fry it up in the pan - and she'll never let you forget you're a man!*" He couldn't remember what was being advertised, but Louie hadn't ever felt more like a man after watching these two go at it. He quickly realized he'd better do something fast, however, as Sheila started to bring the pan down again. He surprised Sheila by darting in and wrenching it away from behind her. He then pressed his gun into her back.

"Alright! Everyone's had their little fun. Drop your weapons and come out where I can see you, or this fine young woman will die right now!"

Tom had just walked out of the freezer and after quickly assessing the situation, dropped the gun he was carrying.

The three bombardiers rose slowly from the back counter and came forward with their hands held high.

"You too!" he barked at Harvey, who was still commandeering a guard with the machine gun. He let the man go and dropped the weapon. The humiliated Iranian turned and threw a haymaker towards Harvey, but Harvey caught his fist and squeezed hard.

"Let him go!" warned Louie, again.

Harvey complied again.

By this time the guard from behind the counter had emerged limping and rubbing his blood-stained pants. The kid, with his captor, came in last.

"Kill them all, Louie!" spat Jazira, staring straight at Sheila, "starting with her first."

"If they knew we were killing people in here, our plan would be completely ruined," countered Louie.

"Coward!" Jazira grabbed the gun at Tom's feet. She held it up to Sheila's head. "If you don't have the balls to do it, then I will!"

Louie moved his gun from Sheila's back to Jazira's head. "If you kill her, all of our plans and our lives will be over. They'll have no restraint to come in here and wipe us all out! Get a hold of yourself, Jazira, she's not worth it."

Jazira seriously thought about the situation for a second.

Chapter Twenty-Two

"**W**hat the hell is going on in here?" yelled Achmed, tearing open the one door left to the kitchen. He had had about enough of not knowing what was going on in the kitchen. He'd left one guard in charge of the others outside. "And you'd better tell me in a hurry why you have a gun pointed at Jazira!"

"She's trying to decide whether it's better to kill this woman and these hostages and bring down the FBI right now on us all, or go on with our plan, Achmed."

Achmed took a breath. "Jazira, don't do it, Louie's right. We won't have any bargaining chips left. You and I won't be able to live out our lives together. Put the gun down, sweetheart."

Jazira slowly put it down, with Louie soon following. As Jazira walked past Sheila out of the kitchen, she threw a sudden vicious punch into Sheila's stomach. Sheila doubled over and Tom ran to help her. He eased her over to the wall and sat her down where she could recover.

"Are you alright?"

"Yeah, I'll be okay," Sheila said, grimacing.

The freezer door opened and out stepped the person Tom had "disciplined." He was bleeding profusely from his temple.

Louie ordered the team medic to patch up everyone who needed it including the guard with the leg wound, and the one who just stumbled out of the freezer.

"What kind of operation are we running around here, the *Bad News Bears* or something?!" Louie asked as he kicked a now half-full sack of flour on the floor, exploding the stuff into the air all over again. "Everyone, get back to your places. I'll stay and help here. Achmed, find Jazira and tell her to get back in here, she'll be cooled off now. Make sure your group is under control and don't let this type of thing happen again."

"Not a chance, Louie." Achmed was off to find Jazira.

....

Sam was still upset his plan of bringing Mrs. Fisher into the situation hadn't panned out. Now, his blood was boiling from a whole lot of gunfire coming from the Oceanside. He didn't waste any time in trying to find out what happened. He was going to give Louie one chance to explain it to him, and if the answer wasn't satisfactory, he and his team were going in no holds barred. He grabbed the speaker.

"Louie, you'd better tell me you're not target practicing on my United States citizens. If you aren't holding up your end of the deal, you won't be a spot on the sand when I get through with you!"

Louie found his megaphone. "Everything's okay in here. Just a little ruckus that needed taking care of. No one is hurt. Everything is going as planned. You just better keep your end of the bargain if you don't want a blood bath on *your* hands."

....

Bortz, Burton, Bunny and the rest of their crew had no idea what was going on. For all they knew, the worst had happened. There was absolutely no way they were going to rush anyone from their vantage point under the deck. There was only one gunmen guarding them now, but his machine gun was trained on them and the only way out from under the deck was directly in front of him. They were sitting ducks. Still, it was the ultimate frustration for Bortz to not know if Harvey was okay.

"Don't do it, Bortz. You don't stand a chance if you try to get out of here. You won't be helping Harvey if you die right here in the sand." Burton was trying to talk some sense to him.

Just then Achmed came back to their group and related the happenings to their guards in Arabic.

"Hey, what happened? Tell us, man, what's going on?!" Bortz yelled, speaking what was on everyone's mind.

Achmed left off talking and bent under the deck. "Nothing we couldn't handle. Seems like we had some unsuccessful heroes. They were easily put down. I'd advise you all to sit quietly tonight. I'm not much in the mood for any other tricks." He moved back out into the night.

PART 4

Chapter Twenty-Three

No one had slept a wink. It was a beautiful Miami morning. Not a cloud in the clear blue sky. A cool ocean breeze was coming in from the south. Sea gulls could be heard in the distance. There were a few fishing boats already offshore. It was a surreal backdrop against the events about to unfold.

Sam was on the roof of the hotel with his binoculars. He and his team were going to be ready for anything. He knew that the government was not going to let any terrorists out of United States airspace - no matter what. If he played his cards right, casualties could kept to a minimum. Whatever the case, he would carry out his duties in their entirety.

He could already hear the drone of the helicopter coming. It was getting louder and louder, breaking apart the pseudo-peaceful Miami morning.

Inside what was left of the Oceanside, plans had been placed in action before sunrise. There was extreme excitement among the captives. They had been rounded up and placed together in the main dining area.

"I have some good news for most everyone," Louie was explaining. "All of you except for one lucky soul will be set free this morning. However, if there is any trouble from any of you, you will not be seeing any of your family members this morning or ever again. Everyone understand?"

The captives nodded in agreement like members of a church choir during a Sunday morning sermon.

"Now, for my next order of business; I need someone for my ace in the hole. Anyone like to travel?" He was striding around the group huddled together in the center of the room. "Aw, come on. No international jet-setters? It's a free trip. You don't even have to use your frequent flyer miles! Iran is especially beautiful this time of year. Sure, you give up a little freedom, but at least there is national health care!" He could see he was not persuading anyone.

"Alright, let's see. You look like someone that the government wouldn't want to shoot down." He grabbed Burton and pulled him from Bunny's arms. Bunny ran after Burton and threw her arms around him sobbing, "Don't take him, please... please don't take him!"

A gunman pulled her off of him and shoved her back into the group. Harvey and Bortz grabbed her and held her for her own protection.

"I'll be okay honey, don't worry. I'll be okay." Burton heard his voice crack as he tried to sound as confident as he could in the situation.

Tom, seeing this being played out, knew what he should do. Sheila knew what Tom was going to do before Tom stepped out.

"Don't do it, Tom, please don't."

"I need to … I have to."

All eyes snapped to Tom as he proclaimed, "I'll do it. Leave him behind, take me - I'm your volunteer."

"Well, what do we have here? A volunteer? Louie's eyes found the person who'd spoken. "The man of the cloth?" An idea struck Louie. "Well, it might do us a little good to have a preacher on board. Maybe he'd be a good luck charm!"

Louie pushed Burton back toward Bunny and the group. He walked up to Tom, looked him up and down and said, "You're exactly the right size, come with me." Louie grabbed his arm and instantly Tom was being led toward the men's restroom with two gunmen close behind.

Burton and Bunny hugged tightly for a long moment. Then, as Louie, Tom, and a couple of gunmen left, Achmed ordered everyone over to the wall closest to the street to sit down and wait. There wasn't a more compliant group of people. Each hoped all this would be over soon.

Sheila was deeply concerned about Tom, however.

Once in the bathroom, Tom noticed there were several vests hanging from the wall. As Louie handed him one, he was instructed to put it on. Louie put one on as well and handed the two others one. They put theirs on. There was a detonator in each pocket. Louie grabbed Tom's out and commanded, "Let's go."

Sheila's fears peaked when she saw Tom being led out of the bathroom with a bomb-vest on. Louie carried small metal boxes in his right hand that she could only guess were detonators.

"Oh my God, Tom, no!" she cried out as they walked past toward the deck.

"It's okay. No matter what happens, God is with me, He'll see me through." He was shoved out the back door and Sheila had grave doubts if she would ever see this brave, kind man again.

Greeting them as they walked out the back door was the gale force sandy wind and deafening noise of a helicopter landing on the beach. Achmed was left to guard the hostages until the last minute. Jazira, Louie, and Tom entered the helicopter. The pilot, as planned, got out and ran through the sand around the building and to safety in the hotel.

After seeing the pilot go past, Achmed commanded the hostages to move to the helicopter and make a circle around it. Everyone was shielding their eyes from the driving sand the helicopter was churning. The guards prodded them along quickly until they surrounded the chopper.

Achmed yelled for his underlings to jump into the craft. Seeing no one move, he realized that with the deafening noise he could not be heard. He motioned for them, getting their attention, and they all jumped in. Lastly, Achmed jumped into the pilot's seat and he lifted the chopper off the ground.

Chapter Twenty-Four

It was a large and open aircraft. Achmed and Jazira were in the front with Jazira as copilot. Louie and Tom were just inside the opening of the passenger section. The others were just behind them. It was crowded with seven people jammed into the passenger area. Tom's eyes burned and his stomach was nauseated with the acidic smell of people who hadn't taken a shower in a very long time.

....

Sam watched as the helicopter lifted off. The first pilot was safe back in the hotel. The FBI was chomping at the bit for the helicopter to get a few miles out to the sea so they could play with some of their toys they hadn't gotten to use in a while. But, Sam had received a very interesting phone call a few hours ago. If Louie had told the truth, there was going to be a surprise ending. Sam told everyone he was going to give the situation a little bit of time before going into full attack mode.

....

Achmed took the helicopter on a low route toward Cuba, where they would have their first stop and had arranged to switch to a private jet to take them along to their final destination of Iran.

Louie is looking very nervous, Tom thought to himself. *God, help this to all work out.*

They were now about a mile out to sea and Louie was sweating much more than his outfit warranted. He looked at Jazira's beautiful but deadly face in the chopper's passenger-view mirror. How could such death come from such a beautifully mesmerizing face? As a boy, his mother had been right to warn him to not hang out with women like her. He looked around at the other Iranians, so happy to be starting the trip back to their homeland, no doubt thinking they were going to receive more money than they'd ever seen. They were laughing and jostling each other in their giddiness. He looked at Tom, beside him, giving up his life for people he'd barely known. He remembered the sad, disapproving look of his mother as she flew off from the Oceanside. Then, floating back into his mind came his recurring dream. Everyone was his friend and enjoyed his company while his star was rising. But when it fell, it was a terrible mess. A single tear ran down his right cheek as he prepared to do something that he knew he was going to do since his talk with his mother. He was going to make her proud.

He looked back toward Jazira. Jazira caught his eye in the mirror and knew something was wrong with him immediately. She turned around and screamed something in Arabic in vain. The engine and blade noise was deafening and no one was even paying attention to her. Achmed, seated beside her, was busy navigating the craft with his headphones on and was oblivious about what was to take place. The others were loudly one-upping each other on what they were going to buy with their fortune back in the homeland. It all happened in a matter of seconds and Jazira could only look on incredulously.

Louie suddenly slammed Tom out of the side of the helicopter. The wind knocked out of him, Tom sailed out of the chopper and fell the fifty feet or so into the water, so fast he never knew what exactly happened. The next thing Jazira saw, her eyes widening in horror, was Louie holding the detonator to his own vest high above his head. His face, looking upward, had turned from a look of anxiety to pure serenity. His tears now formed two lines down both cheeks.

"God, forgive me for I have sinned. . . way too many times. This is for you, my dear, sweet mother." These were Louie's last words before detonating himself, obliterating the rest of the crew, and sending the helicopter plummeting toward the ocean in a burning inferno.

EPILOGUE

"This post-terrorist attack party was a great idea to bring closure to an insane couple of days for everyone," remarked Harvey to Burton. They were both standing on Burton's deck, overlooking the Atlantic Ocean. Everyone had just come from a dinner the police department and the city of Miami threw for Sam. It was to honor him for his excellent handling of the hostage situation a week ago. It had also doubled as his retirement celebration. Most of the other ex-hostages were there as well, including the Texans and the Japanese couple, who all had flown in for the special night of honoring Sam and the get-together afterwards. The only one who couldn't make it was Sheila, who had felt that she needed to be by Chance's side for as much time as he had left.

"Yeah, sometimes it just feels good to be alive, Harvey." Burton paused. "You know, I've thought about our conversation several times on the way to the restaurant that night. Do you remember it?"

"Yeah, I think you were extolling the virtues of your lifestyle."

Burton looked embarrassed. "I think I've missed what's important in life for quite a few years. Maybe I've never understood it. He looked back through the wall of glass at all the people having a good time in his living room. "The best things in life, money can never buy."

"You've got a great point there," replied Harvey, as Bortz, Sadie, and Heather came through the sliding door toward them. Heather gave Harvey the drink she had gotten for him. "I know what you mean." Harvey winked at Heather.

"What are you guys talking about?" Heather asked smiling.

"Can you belch your ABCs?" asked Burton with a grin.

"Given the right people and circumstances!" Heather laughed. "Why do you ask?"

Just then, Tom and Sam opened the door and joined them.

"Here are the heroes of the hour!" exclaimed Bortz, clapping them on the back.

"Tom's the true hero, not me," said Sam humbly.

"Well, I owe you one, Tom. A big fat one. Can you believe this guy - he doesn't even want me to do anything for him," Burton complained to everyone, frustrated.

"I've been thinking about that, Burton. I really don't need anything, but I do have a friend that is in a real tight spot right now...."

....

Sheila was in Chance's bed at Miami Children's Hospital, holding him close. She was singing one of the songs her mother had sung to her many nights when she was scared. Chance was going through a more dark time than she had ever experienced. The doctors had done all they could do to help him recover.

Chance interrupted the sweet strain.

"Momma, if I don't make it through my sickness, what is going to happen to me when I die?" Chance asked, his voice weak. His innocent eyes studied his mother's with unquestioning faith and devotion.

Sheila looked down at him, her heart breaking.

"Let's not talk about such things right now, Chance. Let's keep focusing on you getting better." She fought back a tear trying to surface.

"I know, but what if things don't go like we want. What if I...what if I do... die? What's going to happen to me?"

"Well, some people, like Tom, our new friend we've just gotten to know, believe that you could go to heaven and be with God. I'm not sure, but I think he might be right."

"I feel like God has been with me the whole time I've been sick. I think His angels are always around me. Sometimes, when you're not here, I feel loved like when you hold me close. It takes away my fear for a while, until I think of leaving you all alone. Then I get scared for you and I hope

171

you would be okay without me. Would you be alright, Momma?"

"Don't you worry about me, Chance. You just focus on getting better. Somehow I'd make it. I always have." She was looking away from his gaze, hoping he didn't notice the hollowness she felt at the thought of not having her son in her life. Instead of letting him see the tears that were starting to drip down her cheeks, she excused herself to use the restroom a few steps away.

As she looked at herself in the mirror, she knew she wouldn't be all right if Chance died. She didn't know if she could ever recover from something like that. She really hadn't even let herself think about the possibility. She had charged the situation head-on and had tried to overcome it with everything she had. She had even sacrificed her own body to try to bring some kind of miracle to Chance. She had nothing left to give and she knew it. She had spent all her money and energy and now she knew Chance's survival was completely out of her hands.

"Mom, since I could be spending quite a bit of time with God soon, do you think it would be okay if we prayed together and asked Him to help me and you, no matter what happens?"

Sheila looked back through the bathroom doorway at her son. He was looking pale to her these days, but also more grown up than ever before. "Sure, Chance. We need help. I need help."

As she walked over to his bed, she noticed the door to the hallway was open. Normally she would've been embarrassed to do such a thing in front of a busy hospital hallway. Today, though, she didn't have the energy to care of the devil himself was eavesdropping. *Screw 'em. This is between Chance and me.* She was exhausted.

Sheila bent over his bed and put his hand in hers. She formulated her words for the most important but simple prayer she had ever prayed.

"God, if You can hear me, You know what Chance has been through. Please don't let him be taken from me. I know it's asking a lot, but help this all to turn out okay."

Chance leaned over the top of his mother's head and hugged it gently in his small arms. His weak voice started as she finished. "God, thank You for sending Your angels to take care of me. No matter what happens to me, please take care of Momma and help her feel Your hugs like I've felt 'em."

That was it. The prayer was over. There was just as much busyness and noisy bustle from the hallway, but none of it seemed to reach into Chance's room. They both stayed in this position for several moments, reflecting on what they had just done and drinking in each other's presence.

Chance's shift nurse soon brought them back to the present. She bounced in, not knowing, at first, what she interrupted. "Are you seeing visitors right now?" she asked. When she saw that Sheila and Chance were having a "moment" together, she hastily added, "Oh, sorry for barging in like that; I can tell him to come back later."

Sheila looked up at her out of her tear-soaked eyes. "Who is it?"

"It's your friend, the priest."

"Oh, Tom's here, Chance. Are you up for any visitors?"

A big smile broke out on Chance's face. "I'd love to see him!"

"He might be just what we need to lighten the mood around here. Yes, send him in." Sheila beckoned to the nurse.

Tom had visited Chance several times since the Oceanside experience. He had found that Chance loved to collect baseball cards, so when he visited he always brought Chance a package of them from the supermarket checkout stand across the street. Chance would look through the prized cards and analyze the stats on each for the rest of the day.

Today, though, Chance noticed that Tom had something different in his hands as he came in. "Watchya' got, Tom?"

"At least let him come in before you pepper him with questions!" scolded Sheila.

"Oh, it's alright." Tom laughed. "This is actually why I came," he said as he handed the envelope to Sheila. "It's some good news that's been long overdue for you and my buddy, Chance, here." He ruffled the boy's hair. "Go ahead, open it."

Sheila quickly opened the envelope and just stared at the contents for several moments. She brought her hand to her mouth. "Oh my God! Who gave this to you, Tom?" Sheila was in shock.

"One of the survivors of our Oceanside ordeal seems to have had a change of heart in how to manage his finances. He sends his best to Chance and hopes that this check will be enough to help stack the odds more in his favor."

"Oh, Tom, this is more than enough to get Chance into the experimental program that holds so much promise for him. I just can't believe it! I've got to go call his doctor right now! I can only pray he'll still take him! She stood up to leave, but the nurse who witnessed all the excitement told her to stay with Chance and she'd call the doctor immediately. The nurse left and everyone talked about the Burtons' generous gift while nervously waiting for her return. After what seemed like an eternity, she came skipping back into the room.

"He said for you to understand that we're getting started late and there are no guarantees for Chance's recovery, but we'll start him on the treatments first thing in the morning, if you wish to proceed!" she exclaimed.

....

One month later....

It was a gorgeous day outside and Tom had just delivered a beautiful sermon on forgiveness. His main text was the time religious leaders dragged a woman, "caught in the act of adultery," before Jesus, wanting to stone her. Jesus had forgiven her, and before telling the woman to go and sin no more, He had said to the woman's accusers, "He who is without sin among you, let him throw a stone at her first." The religious leaders had all walked away. Tom felt that this sermon had particularly resonated with his audience today.

Tom had always preached to a full house, but since the well-publicized terrorist extravaganza had taken place, with him at the center, every service was standing room only. He liked to joke with other priests that they should throw their church growth manuals away and get into a terrorist skirmish or two.

He was now finished and ready to dismiss everyone in prayer when several people in the back parted and let a woman through, pushing a bald young boy in a wheelchair. Tom instantly recognized Sheila and Chance. Sheila had told him that she would come some day, and she had made good on her promise.

As she got past the others, his chest swelled with hope. Sheila walked the last few paces down the center aisle to Tom and he stepped down the four steps of the stage to meet her.

"Do you think He's got room for one more wayward woman?"

"I think He's been waiting for this day - I know I have." Tom grinned, knowing his patient and loving efforts to help Sheila had finally paid off.

Pretending like he was looking around all over the auditorium for something, Tom added, "I don't see anyone with any stones." He put his arm around her and turned her around to face the congregation.

"I want everyone to meet two very special people. This is Sheila and her son, Chance. You know them as the mother who had the son undergoing experimental brain cancer treatments. You have all been so generous when we have collected money in times past for their needs. I'm so excited to report to you that Chance's brain tumor is now shrinking and he is home with his mother."

The crowd erupted with applause and Sheila saw many people with tears of happiness for her and Chance. Instead of feeling condemned, to her surprise, she actually felt acceptance. When the excitement died down, Tom asked everyone to greet Sheila and Chance before leaving and get to know them. He had a good idea they would be seeing a lot more of them in the coming weeks. After dismissing the service, Tom gave Sheila a big hug and was the first to welcome her and Chance home.

CPSIA information can be obtained at www.ICGtesting.com
Printed in the USA
LVOW120355200412

278409LV00001B/3/P